OVER THE SEA TO DEATH

OVER THE SEA TO DEATH

GWEN MOFFAT

Charles Scribner's Sons
New York

Lovers of the Cuillin will see a similarity between Glen Brittle and Glen Shira but this is merely a matter of topography. The house and inhabitants of Glen Shira have been created by me and the latter bear no resemblance to anyone, alive or dead, in Glen Brittle.

G. M.

Copyright © 1976 Gwen Moffat

Library of Congress Cataloging in Publication Data

Moffat, Gwen.
Over the sea to death.

I.   Title.
PZ4.M69630v3   [PR6064.04]   823'.9'14   76-22472
ISBN 0-684-14808-0

1 3 5 7 9 11 13 15 17 19 C/C 20 18 16 14 12 10 8 6 4 2

Printed in the United States of America

Pronunciation of Gaelic Place Names

Sgurr an Fheadain—Sgurr an Aityan
Coire a' Ghreadaidh—Corrie a' Greeta
Sgurr Dearg—Sgurr Jerrack
Loch Coruisk—Loch Coroosk
Sgurr Mhic Coinnich—Sgurr Vic Coynich
Gars Bheinn—Garsven

Chapter 1

THERE WAS A touch of frost in the night and the tin hut was too cold for any of them to sleep properly. At intervals she heard the two fellows talking and at dawn they got up and left without saying goodbye, but then she didn't really know them. She'd been walking down the glen last night thinking that if no car picked her up, she'd have to keep walking or sleep there, on the grass verge, when she'd come to the roadmen's hut. She'd smelt the pot first and thought it must be campers but someone was smoking inside the hut.

She was lucky; they hadn't welcomed her with enthusiasm but they'd let her sleep inside. They weren't interested in her, probably because she was wearing a big coat and, except for her voice, was indistinguishable in the dark from anyone else on the road.

Owls called all night and she would have liked to close the door but was afraid she might antagonise the men. It was getting light when they left, the owls stopped, and she went to sleep.

She woke late. The sun was up and the hut was stifling. Already the tourists were on the road and cars were rushing past the door.

She sauntered outside combing her hair, and looked around. Vast mountains walled the glen and there was a river below the road. Clumsily, sliding off tussocks in her flip-flops, she reached the water and washed her face with her hands.

After she'd packed her gear, she moved down the glen before she started hitching because if she stayed by the hut, motorists might think there was a fellow inside, waiting while she thumbed the cars.

7

Willie MacNeill, returning from the cattle market, saw her in the distance, one hand up to the brim of a floppy hat, and the breeze flapping her jeans. She was tall and slim and looked, for one moment, incredibly exciting until he realised she wasn't half-naked but wearing a halter top, very dull, like a faded rose.

He took his foot off the accelerator. He assumed she was a motorist whose car had broken down; he'd have thought twice about picking up a hippy.

She told him her name was Terry Cooke—and that she'd had no breakfast, so he stopped at the next inn and she wolfed a pile of sandwiches. He speculated on her age. He was nineteen and he thought she had a child's eyes but she wasn't a child because of her body. She could be eighteen. She told him she was going to Glen Shira.

'We farm there,' he said, 'the old man and me. I'm always picking up lassies who are going to the hostel.'

Her eyes dwelt on his wide shoulders. 'What time will we be there?'

'I'll no' be in Shira till late. I've to go to Portree and pick up the groceries. I'll be after putting you down at Sligachan and you'll have a walk of a few miles.' He added hopefully, 'Or you can spend the evening with me. Saturday night's wild on Skye.'

'I've got a fellow waiting for me in Glen Shira.'

'Who?'

'You're impertinent.'

She turned her shoulder, and the brim of the hat hid her face. He flushed and gripped the wheel. Her spine was a little damp and the pale hair clung to it. He wondered how she dared to wear that top in the Highlands.

'You didn't say that when I was after buying the sandwiches.'

She turned round but he wouldn't look at her.

'I thought those were a gift.'

'They were.' He felt like a small boy.

'Then don't charge me for them.'

After a while she went on, conversationally, 'I expect the girls spoil you.' When he still wouldn't respond she remarked

8

pleasantly, 'Don't be childish. You know you shouldn't be right up this guy's arse. You're a big bully. Drop back and drive how you were driving before.'

'What do you know about driving?'

'I've been with a lot of drivers.'

'I'm damty sure you have.'

She stared at him but he kept his eyes on the road, allowing the space to lengthen between the car ahead and his lorry.

'I don't sleep with all the fellows who pick me up.' She was gently reproving.

'How many then?'

'Just the ones I like.'

'The ones *you* like!'

She laughed. 'How old-fashioned you are!' Then she murmured apologetically: 'No, it's not that; I guess I was right the first time: too many youth hostellers, that's what it will be. Rather unsophisticated?' The tone was engaging and the words anathema. In Willie's book you insulted a woman by inferring that she was a whore but with this one he'd sent off a boomerang. His instinct was to put his foot down and hurl his truck round the corners, but that would only frighten the tourists. She'd look at him with those big dark eyes and smile. He drove on carefully, seething with impotence.

At the Kyle of Lochalsh she got down from the cab and stalked round the quay like an inquisitive cat. In front of the first car in the queue, the ramp that was the end of the road ran straight into the sound, while across the water stood the Isle of Skye. It meant nothing to Willie, but the girl was fascinated by everything. She laughed at the cormorants that dived with a flash of backside and webbed black feet, to pop up yards away, gulping fish. She was enchanted with the rank of varnished East Coasters tied up for the weekend, with the buildings crowding the quay, functional but not displeasing, with the ferry and its crew. The crew studied her dispassionately.

'Those birds are like wee devils,' she remarked on the ferry, catching the idiom, watching a cormorant scooting past their bows. Willie winced. On the island people believed in devils.

'It's hot,' he grumbled, and it was sweltering in the cab.

'I love it hot. When you're on the road and it rains, there's nowhere to dry your clothes, and warm wet stuff smells horrible, and your hair's in rats' tails. You look like death and no one will give you food. Besides, you never feel so hungry in the sun.'

They rolled off the ferry, up another ramp and through the village of Kyleakin to open country. The island was grey in the drought: pewter and smeared silver, hazed by the heat, with the air above every rock shivering as if in a mirage. The odd cottage, dazzling in this soft light, drowsed through the afternoon. An occasional tourist car drifted by, or could be glimpsed, stationary, in the shade of scrub birches.

There was another place, a town he called it, and she thought he was joking: another collection of white-washed houses, a couple of stores, a garage and an hotel. In a moment they were past it, and strange hills loomed ahead while on their right were islands and water and, on the other side of the sound, the mainland hills. They ran under immense slopes of scree where she had to bend down to see the top, and round lochs like fiords with birds feeding on the exposed mud. A smell of seaweed filled the cab.

The scree slopes receded, opening out to moorland, and away on their left, spiky peaks were a frieze without detail against the sky. Between these and the road, the moor descended in random steps, gleaming like glass in places where water ran over slabs. Now, ahead of them, was a junction and a long rambling building in the ubiquitous whitewash under a jumble of slate roofs. It appeared uninhabited.

'Is anyone left alive on Skye?' she wondered aloud. 'Perhaps they all died suddenly and left just us.'

'This is Sligachan,' he announced, slowing down, then coaxingly: 'Come in and have a drink with me.'

She returned his look coolly. 'I'll wait.'

He had nice lips but his smile could be cruel. 'I'm no' going farther.'

Her eyes widened, then, without a word, she started to gather

her things together. Such ready acceptance made him feel guilty.

'I told you,' he reminded her, 'I'm no' going straight to the glen; I've to go to Portree. I'm coming back this way if you'll wait—or you can come with me.'

'I'll walk.'

'Don't be like that. Wait for me. I'll no' be long.'

'Can't I walk to Glen Shira from here?'

'It's eight miles!'

She climbed down from the cab and wrinkled her nose at the smell of beer from the bar. 'Which road do I take?'

He shrugged. 'You go round the side of the building and up the Dunvegan road a ways. On the left there's a signpost.'

'Thanks.' She put the string of the bedding roll round her neck.

'Hell!' he protested. 'You're no' going to walk over the moor carrying that stuff! Let me take it in the wagon.' She gave him an indulgent smile and picked up her carrier bags. 'Why don't you have a rucksack?' he asked desperately.

'You're obsessed with youth hostellers.'

He glanced at the sky; it was an adult look but his tone was sulky. 'If you don't come down the glen tonight, I'm no' turning out for you. You've got a sleeping bag; you'll need to crawl under a rock till daylight but you've nothing to fear on the moor. No one's after dying of exposure in this weather. It'll be a fine night.'

He turned and swaggered into the bar. She hesitated for a moment then started walking.

He was rather sweet, she thought, for a farm boy; he hadn't lost his bloom yet. He seemed kind. He didn't like being snubbed yet his retaliation wasn't spiteful but quick and natural. Terry knew that she roused strong reactions but she found it difficult to distinguish between people whom she charmed and those she repelled, or at least disturbed. If she sometimes suspected that not everyone found her irresistible, then she knew an increased thrill, but if she was aware of danger it was only as an extension of excitement. She was sixteen and had survived so long through luck.

She thought about Willie's husky body—and of George. But George was old; fellows couldn't be expected to keep their bodies hard indefinitely, and he'd had a lot of falls. Besides, he didn't look after himself; it was a bad diet, not age, had made George put on weight. Certainly he was nearer forty than the thirty-six he claimed.... Suddenly the thought occurred to her that when she was thirty-six and thus already old, George would be around sixty, if he were still alive. She wasn't sure whether she was more shocked at the thought of George as a very old man, or of his dying—but then he could be killed at any time. He'd pointed that out himself, the first time he'd met her. She'd thought then what a terrible thing that was to have to live with.

She dawdled, her flip-flops scuffing in the gravel. She felt hot and sweaty and very much alone. She stopped and looked back at the hotel Willie called Sligachan. George was eight miles away and this one was so near—and so much more accommodating. She remembered the warm eyes on the other side of the cab, the hard chest under the shirt. She bit her lip and sighed. George said she was over-sexed and she supposed he was right because you couldn't be all that old without acquiring some wisdom about girls. She resumed her trudge up the road, looking now at the mountains from under the brim of her hat. Her gaze ranged over the moor and the weird skyline, and came back to a signpost which read, 'Footpath to Glen Shira' and seemed to be pointing to an empty world.

'God, it's creepy,' she whispered. 'I should have stayed with Willie.'

'Why are we stopping?' Lavender Maynard's voice had a cutting edge.

'Because I can't look at the scenery while I'm driving, dear.'

Her husband reversed into the big lay-by at the head of Glen Shira and switched off. He peered through the windscreen and sighed. 'Too hazy.'

'The place to stop is above the hairpins,' Lavender pointed out. 'You can see only one corrie from here.'

'That's the one that matters,' he murmured absently.

Her dark glasses were turned on him. 'Why does that corrie matter?'

'Because we can see the Lindsays' route from here; could do, with decent visibility. Mustn't grumble in an anti-cyclone—'

'Madge Fraser's route, you mean.'

'Yes, dear; they took both guides today.'

'But I suppose you'll pay her all the same?'

'Naturally. I engaged her for the fortnight; I don't deduct a day's fees because you insist on my taking you to Portree shopping.'

'So she'll pick up double wages today. Easy money.'

He regarded her angular body without expression. 'She earns every penny of it. Can you suggest an occupation which is more dangerous—or which gives so much pleasure to the client?'

Her hands twitched in her lap but she said with deliberation, 'I shouldn't think danger has much, if any significance, where people of low intelligence are concerned.'

After a moment he said reflectively, 'You could have a thought there—quite a thought.'

'Where are you going?'

'Just getting out, dear, for a breath of fresh air.'

Leaning against the bonnet, feeling the hot metal through his slacks, he looked up the corrie and thought that somewhere within visual distance the Lindsays and their two guides were scrambling carefully along the crest of the ridge, or descending some easy gully close behind Madge, with George bringing up the rear. He saw them in his mind's eye, stop and cluster: about a late saxifrage perhaps, or to gape at a basking viper. Madge didn't care much for wildlife but she knew what her clients wanted.

His gaze wandered leftwards across vast wastes of rock and moor to the pass that led to Sligachan. His eyes narrowed. Someone was coming along the path: strung with packages and walking with difficulty.

'Shall we go on for tea?' Lavender's voice hinted at urgency. She liked her tea at five o'clock and it was now ten to.

13

'Hold on a minute; this girl looks at the end of her tether. We might offer her a lift.'

'Do we have to get involved with every slut in Glen Shira?'

'Oh, for Christ's sake!' He went and leaned on the driver's door. 'All right,' he said soothingly, 'I know it's been a trying day but it was you who wanted to go shopping. I did warn you that Portree would be hell on Saturday afternoon—'

'All you wanted to do was climb—'

'It's what I came here for—'

'I don't climb, Kenneth.' Softly.

'You didn't have to come, dear.'

'No. And you'd have preferred me to stay at home so that you could come to Skye and take up with Madge Fraser where you left off—'

Her voice shrilled dangerously but he was walking away: up the road to the end of the Sligachan path, trying to shut out the tirade, peering at the limping traveller—then he smiled incredulously, for this was out of the frying pan and into the fire with a vengeance. No wonder Lavender was hysterical; she had better eyesight than he.

She was fabulous: long-waisted, long-legged, wearing pants which made her look like a fashion plate, a pink halter top and a big blue hat. The legs of the pants should have been a riot of little flowers but they were smeared by peat stains to the knees. Even in a drought the inexperienced ones always found the bogs. She carried a bedding roll and a shoulder bag, huge plastic holdalls and a pair of flip-flops.

He exclaimed in horrified amusement, 'You've never walked from Sligachan like that?'

She stopped and put down her bags. Her expression was friendly and apologetic.

'I thought the path would be better. I don't know why I should have done. It didn't seem far: eight miles, but I haven't seen a soul, not even in the distance!'

'You've only done five miles; you've got three to go to civilisation—such as it is. But not now,' he added hastily, seeing her alarm, 'I'll take you to the hostel. Why are you limping?'

14

She sat down in the heather and presented the sole of one foot: clean from the bogs, but the thick skin gashed by glass or tin. Blood started to ooze from the wound.

'Don't you carry any Elastoplast, woman?' She shook her head. 'No First Aid at all?'

She smiled winningly. 'I can make it to your car; I can see you're the kind of guy who always carries First Aid stuff.'

He regarded her lugubriously and his voice was sad. 'So right you are. Come along then. You won't lean on me?' He glanced towards the car. 'You may be wise. My wife is a little tired,' he told her after some yards of slow progress. 'What's your name?'

'Terry Cooke.'

'Mine's Ken Maynard, and this—' as they came within speaking distance of Lavender's window, '—is my wife. Will you hand me the First Aid box, my dear, and unlock the rear door?'

Wordlessly, Lavender did as he asked, the dark glasses turned on the girl with anonymous menace. Ken muttered to himself as he dressed the foot and re-packed the First Aid box. Then he stowed the girl's gear beside her and climbed into the driver's seat.

'You're going to the youth hostel.'

It was a casual assumption. His hand moved to the ignition key but he was looking at the mountains across the glen.

'I'm going to the camp site.'

He twisted in his seat. 'Meeting someone there?'

'That's hardly our business,' Lavender observed pointedly.

'You don't seem to be able to take care of yourself,' he grumbled. Suddenly, back in the car, he felt a wave of claustrophobia and remembered that he'd lost a day's climbing—at his age never to be recovered. It couldn't be recovered at any age, but time was unbelievably precious once one had passed fifty.

'I guess, when I throw myself on your mercy like this,' Terry was saying, 'that it could be your business what becomes of me.'

'You're making us responsible for you?' Lavender asked in

astonishment. Maynard switched on the ignition and started down the road.

'Hell,' the girl said. 'Old people are always getting in a state about me.'

He winced but recovered quickly. 'They've got good cause. Suppose the mist had come down on the moor. What would you have done?'

'It wouldn't. I got a lift with a fellow who lives here and he said it would stay fine tonight. Anyway, he'd have come and looked for me.'

'How enchanting. What fellow was that?'

'Willie MacNeill.'

'Oh, Lord!' His eyes met hers in the mirror and she winked at him. 'How old are you?' he asked curiously.

'Nineteen.' She was prim.

Lavender asked coolly: 'What are you proposing to do in Glen Shira?'

'I'm joining a friend.'

'Another one?'

In the silence he thought: Go on: elaborate, dear. Tell the girl you meant she's being passed from hand to hand....

Terry was saying pleasantly: 'I didn't know Willie before he picked me up. The only friend I've got here is the one I've come to see.'

'You're wrong there,' he said firmly, 'you've got me.'

Lavender gasped. '*What?*'

'This child,' he said with mock-seriousness, 'is one of Nature's innocents. And this glen—' he glanced at his wife and he wasn't smiling, '—in a heat-wave, is a curious place.' But he chuckled at Terry in the mirror and she smiled a little wearily. 'You don't know Skye, do you? There are some funny people in Glen Shira, my dear; you could do with one more friend than the one you have already, you particularly.' He paused, wondering if she was aware of her own beauty. 'Who is he, by the way?' No one thought of Terry as having women friends.

'His name's George Watkins. Do you know him?'

Lavender turned again and stared at her. 'The guide?'

'Yes. You do know him then?'

'We know him.' Ken's voice was flat. 'Like I said: you need friends, dear.'

Chapter 2

MELINDA PINK, J.P. was sitting in her modest Austin at the top of the ramp leading down to the Sound of Sleat. Hers was the first car in the queue and standing beside her open window was a young man with flowing hair restrained by a brow-band which, with his deep tan and sombre eyes and the fact that the hair was silky and bleached almost white, gave him the air of a Palomino pony. Beside him on the cobbles was a tall heavy pack. He had old boots creamed with dust, and his breeches had seen better days. Under a ragged tartan shirt he wore a pendant in twisted metal on a leather boot-lace.

Miss Pink had exchanged a few words with him about the heat and the difficulty shown by a cormorant in trying to swallow a flatfish, and now, pouring tea from her flask, she invited him to share it. He accepted, and surveyed the contents of the car: the olive anorak on the back seat, a small, practical rucksack. His eyes considered her cropped grey hair and owlish spectacles.

'Are you climbing?' he asked tentatively.

'I'm going to Glen Shira. Can I give you a lift?'

With alacrity he stowed his pack in the boot and settled himself in the passenger's seat. A strong odour of sweat came in with him. He said he had been climbing on Ben Nevis for two days and that he had a cottage in Glen Shira. She asked him if he lived on Skye all the year round.

'No, just for the summer.' There was a pause. 'I do some guiding when I can get the custom.' He caught her quick look and smiled. 'I'm not certificated.' When she made no comment he continued, 'Do you think guides should be slaves to bits of paper?'

18

'You've got to protect the public. I'm strongly against incompetent men setting themselves up as guides and putting foolish clients at risk. The public is extraordinarily trusting where dangerous activities are concerned.'

'There are bad guides.'

'Qualified, you mean? With certificates?'

'Oh yes.'

He was grim. Miss Pink's mental ears were pricked. 'Have you engagements in Glen Shira now?' she asked casually.

'A couple of days next week. It's been a long season and I've been lucky. I had a day with a guy from Glen Shira House last week. He arrived early and had booked Madge Fraser for a fortnight but she asked me to take him till she was free. Do you know Madge?'

'I don't know her; I've heard of her, of course. Does she live in the glen?'

'She's not resident there. She moves about, like me—like all of us.' There was that grim note in his voice again. 'She's spent most of this season in Scotland: the Ben, Glen Coe, Skye. I go out with her occasionally. She's good.'

'Ah.' Miss Pink turned interested eyes on him. 'Who leads?'

'We lead through a lot.'

'Who leads the hard pitches?'

'She's a good all-round mountaineer,' he said firmly, 'but she admits herself that she's no great rock climber.'

Miss Pink regarded the approaching ferry in astonished silence. All climbing was relative and she would have said that the routes which Madge Fraser had to her credit were very fine climbs indeed, so if this man were better, then he was good.

The ferry docked and she was waved down the ramp and across the deck. She switched off the ignition and they stared through the windscreen at the ruined castle on the other side of the sound.

'Who did you say her client was?'

'This man I had earlier, Ken Maynard. He's a bouncy little guy, lives only for climbing, and there's nothing he won't tackle.

He could never lead, of course, which is why he takes guides, but he's a competent second. Great company on the hill, too.'

As he talked his mobile face shone with enthusiasm and she thought what a happy contrast he was with some of the young men she saw in the courts. Aloud she said, 'I met Mr Maynard last year in the Lakes. You didn't tell me your name.'

'Colin Irwin.'

'Mine is Pink. I live in Cornwall.'

'Do you?' His eyes lit up again. 'I'm from Stranraer; *our* sea cliffs are just vertical tips.'

'Granite is delightful,' she enthused, 'but at rather a high angle when one is getting on. I have to lower my standard on Cornish cliffs.'

'Have you been climbing up here?'

'I've just had two weeks in Sutherland and Wester Ross. If you're free tomorrow you might like to take me up something.'

'I'd be delighted.'

They discussed the relative merits of Skye climbs and he filled in the gaps in her memory. It was many years since she'd visited Glen Shira. She had booked a room at the only hotel and now she asked him if he knew the proprietor: Mr Hamlyn.

'*Mister* Hamlyn,' he repeated, savouring it, and smiled. 'Everyone in the glen calls him "the colonel". Yes, I know him: not to speak to, of course; he wouldn't acknowledge me. He's been brought up in the tradition of alpine guides: a very formal crowd, call their clients "sir" and all that.' He grinned mischievously. 'Keep their hair short.'

'Yes,' Miss Pink said. 'But it's not the appearance, is it? It's those certificates. Regular Servicemen have etiquette drilled into them. Does he still climb?'

'Occasionally. Not with me of course.'

'With Madge Fraser?'

'Yes. Not with Watkins.' She said nothing. 'George Watkins,' he elaborated without expression. 'He's the other guide in the glen.'

'Why doesn't Colonel Hamlyn go out with him?'

He looked out of his window. 'Everything's as dry as a bone,' he observed. 'That waterfall has hardly anything in it.' Then, carelessly: 'Watkins and the colonel? I guess they don't get on.' After a moment he asked: 'What does Ken Maynard do?'

'He edits a woman's magazine.'

'That explains a lot. I thought he was trying to escape from something.' He sighed and his eyes followed a cockerel which suddenly raced across the road to a barn. 'His wife's very unhappy,' he added gravely. Miss Pink slowed for a cow suckling its calf in the middle of the road. 'Funny lot,' he went on. 'Then there are the Lindsays. They're with Watkins,' he added tightly.

'Who are the Lindsays?'

'Oh, another couple. But they both climb. Mrs Maynard doesn't, you see. Perhaps that's the trouble. But both the Lindsays climb.' He was abstracted again. 'That may be their trouble.'

Ahead of them Sligachan Hotel showed at the junction of the Portree and Dunvegan roads. Miss Pink continued west, across the centre of the island at its narrowest point, and after a few miles they came to the hamlet of Drynoch.

Below them now was Loch Harport, filling up with the tide, so full in fact that the water had pushed a trio of heron back to the weed-line. Miss Pink stopped and the birds rose and flapped lazily up the course of a burn to fish in lochans on the moor.

'Midges are biting,' she remarked, putting the car in gear. One didn't halt for long beside a Skye loch on a September evening.

She drove up the hill to the Shira road-end, turned hard left, and as they crossed the high moor, she watched the peaks of the Cuillin come into view, gauzy and dreaming in the sun, with the two splendid corries separated by the cone of Sgurr an Fheadain where Waterpipe Gully was a pencilled line on the rock.

The road was narrow but where it dipped to descend steeply to the glen, there were wide hairpins, then the way reverted to a single track with passing places marked by white diamonds on posts. She remembered that somewhere about here was the start of the path going over to Sligachan. On the right was a big lay-by with a forestry track behind a gate. Below them the river bed was a string of boulders with hardly a gleam of water visible from a distance. On the other side of the glen long scree slopes ran to the top of the only dull peak in Glen Shira. A drift of warm air spiced with resin came through the open windows.

They crossed the river by way of a wooden bridge which rattled under the wheels. Now the road twisted among heathery humps and far ahead the sky seemed brighter and the light of a different cast: softer perhaps, as if it held another quality from that inland—if anywhere could be termed inland on an island that was nowhere more than a few miles from the sea.

A tall square structure appeared: the youth hostel. Figures moved about it: all young except for an elderly collie. There were towels and swim suits on washing lines, and a few dusty cars. Cattle replaced sheep on the road, and the woods of Glen Shira came into view: sycamores and birches with the odd redwood spired above the canopy. From road-level the trees hid the mouth of the glen and, but for the curious light and the tang of weed (scarcely noticed because it is seldom lost on the island), one would never have guessed that the Atlantic lay within half a mile.

Irwin asked to be set down before they reached the woods. 'That's my place.' He indicated a shabby cottage on the far bank of the river. 'That's Largo,' he added with pleasure. 'Maybe I'll go out and get some fish for supper.'

'It'll soon be dark.'

He smiled. 'But that's nice: fishing in the dark. I'll take you out one night.'

After she'd dropped him she continued to a gateway and a notice by a cattle grid which said, GLEN SHIRA HOUSE PRIVATE. A gravel drive wound through glades where sycamore trunks sprouted lichen like plastic lettuce leaves. As a walled garden came in view on her left, the trees thinned and the house appeared, raised a few feet on a knoll. It was shabby, large and roughly square, with a porch crowned by concrete castellations.

A figure moved behind a window and a man stepped out on the gravel sweep.

Miss Pink, suddenly assuming the protective role of the elderly spinster and blinking with what might have been nervousness, saw a tall and well-preserved man in his sixties who, from his bearing, could only be the colonel: Lieutenant Colonel Gordon Hamlyn (Rtd). He wore a soft shirt the colour of mud, a club tie and shapeless trousers in expensive tweed. His hair was short and his moustache clipped. His eyes were blue and he regarded her with a belligerent stare. The impression was that he was over-playing the role and she could only pray that he would turn out to be amusing.

He gave a welcoming bark. 'Miss Pink, ma'am! We are delighted to see you safe and sound.' She felt as if she'd galloped down the Khyber in front of Afghan hordes. She blinked at a string of molehills on the lawn and said she was delighted to be there.

He carried her bags upstairs. The walls were hung with swords and sabres, daggers, a pair of Gurkha kukri, various firearms. He showed her to her room and retreated with a flourish, bowing. She suspected that she was the oldest guest and he assumed he'd found a kindred spirit.

They had put her on a south-west corner and she had two windows; one, a bay with a window seat, looked over the lawn and a meadow to miles of shining sea, the Isle of Canna and the cliffs of Rum. Through the other she was startled to see Colin Irwin, across the river, feeling for the key above the lintel of Largo's door. She watched him enter, to emerge in a moment without his pack and carrying a bucket. He went to a burn which, from this distance, was nothing more than a line of stones. On its northern bank the conifers, which stretched all the way down the western side of the glen, climbed to the skyline.

She turned to her room. One corner had been partitioned for a bathroom which was in itself commodious, yet it left enough space that the massive Victorian furniture was not obtrusive. The colour scheme was off-white with touches of plum and sage-green. The ceiling was high, drawers ran as if on ball bearings, the bath water was scalding hot. There remained only the food. That, and the colonel's lady, were unknown quantities. So were the other guests, but at the moment Miss Pink's thoughts were concentrated on her dinner and she hoped devoutly that Mrs Hamlyn could cook.

It was no forlorn hope. As she went downstairs there was a smell of herbs, hot wine and roasting mutton. She was in nice time for sherry. Voices guided her to a large room with a wide window and a bar. A group of people stood at the bar and a man detached himself, extending his hand. She recognised Ken Maynard.

He introduced her to his wife, a thin woman perched with a youthful air on a bar stool. Lavender Maynard might have been a striking redhead once but now her hair was deeply tinted above the face of an ageing squirrel. She wore a bright green jersey sheath which emphasised her sharp angles distressingly.

The other woman in the room was introduced as Betty Lindsay. She was large and solid with a loud voice, lavish gestures and unquiet eyes. Her husband was small and preoccupied. As he took Miss Pink's hand, his lips did little more than twitch in the semblance of a smile.

She accepted sherry from Maynard and remarked that she understood Madge Fraser was staying at the hotel. He nodded, his warm brown eyes fixed on hers. Behind him Lavender stiffened. Miss Pink realised that she should have tested the temperature first. Her eyes wandered vaguely to Hamlyn who was emptying an ash tray. Betty Lindsay said: 'The energy of that girl! And she's not all that young—'

'And a mother.' For some reason, perhaps an impediment, Lavender threw her voice so that every syllable appeared to be jerked out of her. At first hearing this was painful and embarrassing, and Miss Pink looked vacuous as she observed that even grandmothers climbed nowadays. She glanced at Hamlyn who responded roguishly.

'In my opinion it is the older people who have the energy, ma'am, but then, they're the ones who enjoy life.' His face fell.

'I'm very depressed when I look at today's youngsters; it's not just their long hair and the terrible manners—it's their aimlessness. We had to work to make our way in the world; these actually *prefer* to live on National Assistance!'

Murmured agreement came from Maynard. 'There's no discipline,' he assured Miss Pink earnestly.

She recognised the game immediately. He was a bear-baiter—but apparently Hamlyn was not unaware of this.

'That's a generalisation,' their host admitted, referring to his own comments, 'not all youngsters are layabouts—' he regarded Maynard distantly, '—not all adults are useful members of society.'

'How right you are,' Lavender put in, addressing the end of her cigarette.

Betty Lindsay came in with a rush: 'You missed a fabulous climb today, Ken. Didn't he, Andy?'

Her husband nodded. She hesitated, then went on, to the company generally: 'Archer Thompson's Route; it's a classic.'

'George didn't think much of it,' Lindsay said.

'Oh, Andy! George was miserable because we had to walk three miles to the cliff! He thought it was wasted climbing time.'

'Rock gymnast,' Hamlyn muttered.

'Gymnast? Watkins?' Maynard was clowning again. 'You have to be joking.'

Lindsay turned on him furiously. 'He leads harder stuff than you'll ever be hauled up!'

'Led them once,' the other corrected, unperturbed. 'In his remote youth. But even there, you've only got his word for it. I doubt if George ever did anything harder than a Severe—with a following wind.'

Betty hooted with laughter. Lindsay's face, which had been quite pale to begin with, was flushed and ugly. Miss Pink moved across the room to contemplate Sgurr Alasdair and Sgumain: a far vista beyond the end of a rough avenue of trees. In the sunset the black rock had a magenta tint and she remained there, staring, while behind her the colonel remarked judiciously:

25

'Watkins was never a brilliant climber, Andrew; I doubt if he would get his certificates in these days. The tests are pretty searching.'

'Are they?' Betty asked brightly. 'What does one have to do? Ah, here's Madge; she'll tell us.'

Miss Pink turned with interest to see a girl in a long white dress, with bare arms and a plunging neckline, who looked like a starlet until one noticed her build. She was lissom but all muscle, and no starlet had the flat arrogance that was in Madge Fraser's eyes. Apart from that she was not remarkable. Her hair curled and was cut short, her features were regular, her ears set flat to her head. She looked chic and very neat. When she was introduced to Miss Pink she referred, and correctly, to one of that lady's exploits in the Alps. Ken Maynard observed this exchange with an air of proprietorial amusement.

Betty Lindsay said, 'What are the qualifications for a guide, Madge?'

The girl frowned. She must have been about thirty but she looked younger. 'I forget what they are technically; I judge the applicants according to whether I think they'll make good guides.'

'*You* judge! What d'you mean: *you* judge?' No one seemed unduly surprised at Lindsay's rudeness, only resigned.

'I'm a senior guide.' Her voice was colourless. 'There's a panel of examiners and I'm on it. We have them on the hill for two or three days and judge their ability; that's all.'

'Why—?' Lindsay began, but Maynard got there first: 'Why isn't George on this panel?'

'Whatever's got into you?' Madge asked and he looked into his drink without answering.

'Well, why isn't he?' Lindsay barked, and Miss Pink wondered how much he'd had to drink this evening.

Madge had no time for Lindsay. 'Because he's not good enough,' she said coldly.

'I'll say one thing for lady guides,' Hamlyn observed quickly, setting a whisky before Madge and addressing no one in particular. 'They're workers: punctual to the minute in the morning, and there's none of this breaking off early and rushing down for opening time as there is with some of the men.'

Madge laughed. 'You don't keep your clients if you short-change them.'

'Some people don't care.' Hamlyn looked hard at her.

'Well,' she said easily, as if this were an old topic, 'hard work's no fun if you don't like the job.' She glanced at Betty carelessly. 'He can't wait for the winter, you know.'

The other nodded agreement. 'He's answered an advert for a handyman in an hotel at Aviemore.'

'I know. Christ!'

Lavender said: 'It wouldn't occur to you, I suppose, that your criticism of a colleague was rather unethical—in public?'

Madge looked at her. 'No.'

Maynard said quickly, 'We brought his girl friend down the glen; picked her up at—'

'George's *girl friend*!' It was Lindsay again. 'What the hell are you talking about?'

As Maynard stared at him, Madge said with interest: 'I didn't know he'd got a girl coming.' She turned to Betty. 'Did you?'

The big woman shook her head dumbly.

'Collects them like flies,' Maynard said. 'You can go down to the shore any night and find all the female campers in George's tent.'

'You're making that up,' Hamlyn said. 'He's usually up here, drinking.'

'I mean afterwards.'

'Tell us about this girl,' Betty urged.

Maynard looked at his wife, then away. 'Very young—' he drew a breath, '—surprisingly beautiful. Not a climber; all strung around with packages, you know the kind of thing; no rucksack.'

Madge shrugged and looked bored. Betty said, 'I can't believe it. Does he know she's coming?'

'I didn't ask her. She walked over the moor in flip-flops.'

'What are flip-flops?' Hamlyn asked.

27

'Sandals with no heels; you keep them on by a bit that goes between the toes.'

'That's asking for trouble: walking over the moor without boots.'

'I hope she stays off the ridge,' Madge remarked, but not as if she cared.

Hamlyn said: 'I'm with you there. If they're going to come to grief, I'm all for them doing it in an accessible place, like the moor or the sea cliffs. Recovery of the body is so much simpler.'

'They also stand a better chance of survival if they don't have to spend the night lying injured on the ridge,' Miss Pink put in.

Hamlyn smiled at her but not apologetically. 'If you knew the problems we have in this glen, ma'am, you'd sympathise. When we first came here all the climbers knew each other, and they climbed carefully and properly: none of these artificial aids and metallic junk like walking ironmongers' shops. They're criminal!' Miss Pink sensed the atmosphere; as with Lindsay's outbursts, the company was resigned, not askance. These people were used to each other. Her expression remained politely attentive. Hamlyn leaned across the bar. 'D'you know, if you leave your rucksack at the foot of a climb, there's a fifty-fifty chance it won't be there when you come down again? There have been thefts from *tents*! In our day, if anything was missing from your tent it was only ever food, and the thief was either a sheepdog or a fox. It couldn't have been anything else. Why, I remember in the forties when that fellow O'Rorke was convicted for stealing a typewriter from an hotel in the Lakes, the scandal shook the climbing world—and he was an Irishman— what could you expect? Now, theft is so common among climbers the police don't trouble to make inquiries, the implication being that we're mad to think our sport might be different from any other. The whole moral fabric of this country is being ripped apart.' He glared round the bar.

Maynard went on, 'And then there's the nude bathing from the shore—'

Hamlyn nodded fiercely at Miss Pink. 'I've protested to the police, I've been down there with a shot gun, threatening to run them off the land—but it's not mine; the foreshore grazing is MacNeill's—and he's—' he broke off as he was pushed from behind by an opening door.

'—no better than he should be,' a cool voice completed for him. A slim woman in a lemon overall came in the back of the bar and greeted them pleasantly, with a smile and a handshake for Miss Pink.

Whereas her husband had the somewhat bloated features of a Blimpish *bon viveur*, Vera Hamlyn had the hooded eyes, the long nose and primped mouth that is termed patrician. She brushed back her grey hair with a fine but greasy hand.

'A large gin for the cook, darling. And what's old MacNeill been up to now?'

'The nude bathing,' Maynard told her meaningly.

'Oh yes.' She shook her head. 'I'm afraid he's a naughty old man.'

'You've got to watch him,' Hamlyn said, placing a gin in front of his wife. 'There are some very young children on that camp site and when the parents are away climbing and don't come down till late, those children run wild. They go too close to MacNeill's place for my peace of mind.'

'Has he ever been in trouble?' Maynard asked. The Hamlyns stared at him. 'For molesting little girls,' he elaborated. 'That's what you meant, wasn't it?'

Vera Hamlyn shook her head vehemently. 'Oh no, I don't think it's like that. Gordon meant you can't be too careful—and there's so much of it these days: even when they're dressed, they're not really, if you see what I mean?' She looked at Miss Pink for assistance. 'It's so different from when we were young, isn't it?' Miss Pink raised her eyebrows in sympathy.

Madge said coldly, 'We don't have to get hung up over a few kids running around loose; they're dying by the score in the rest of the world. Everyone's got to take a chance, even young kids.'

'It's because this danger is near home,' Vera protested. 'After all, Madge, if it were your child on the shore. . . .' She looked doubtfully at the guide.

'That's what I was thinking of,' Madge said with a trace of anger. 'Don't rile me.'

'Well, there you are, you see.' Hamlyn stared at her in ridiculous triumph.

'All right! Malcolm's a dirty old man and the children on the camp site are at risk. I couldn't care less. When are we eating?'

'Five minutes,' Vera said. 'Did you have a good day, Ken?'

'Yes. We brought another little girl into the glen. George Watkins' dolly.'

'A friend of George's? Did he know she was coming?'

'Not the way he's been behaving.' He looked at Miss Pink speculatively. 'You're always running into trouble; it looks as if this time is going to be no exception.'

Lavender smiled thinly. 'I don't think the type of peccadillo you've been discussing would have any interest for Miss Pink. She's concerned with basics. Like murder.'

Chapter 3

DINNER WAS *table d'hôte* but no one was going to grumble at a saddle of mutton flavoured with thyme and red currants and something which was certainly not cooking wine. Pleasantly replete, they drifted back to the cocktail lounge for coffee and Miss Pink found herself at a table in the window with the Lindsays.

Betty asked if she would like a liqueur and relayed the information to her husband as if he were a waiter, but a poor one. Betty's smile became fixed as he failed to respond.

'Shall I get them, sweetie? You look tired.'

He started, gave them a tremulous smile devoid of context, and turned to the bar.

'It's the heat,' Betty told Miss Pink firmly. 'We've been here a week and we've not missed one day's climbing. We're living on our nerves.'

'There's always a compulsion to make the most of an Indian summer. When the weather breaks here, the rain could last for weeks.'

'And he suffers terribly with indigestion; the doctor thinks it's an ulcer.'

Miss Pink looked grave. 'The pace of modern life ... so exhausting ... but a holiday in Glen Shira should do wonders for him.'

'Yes.' Betty sounded doubtful. 'I think it's time he retired. He's a builder, and with the housing position such as it is, we ought to get out while the going's good. We could afford to retire, particularly if we sold our house and moved to Skye.

Living's so much cheaper up here, and property's going for a song. We could amuse ourselves by buying ruins and doing them up. We can both do the practical work: brick-laying, roofing and so on. We'd employ some labour, of course.'

Miss Pink studied her with renewed interest. She was wearing a long skirt in the dark Lindsay tartan and a plain navy blouse. She looked competent and very powerful.

'Why don't you move?' she asked curiously. 'You sound as if you could make an ideal life for yourselves on the island.'

The other gave her a meaning glance. 'We will.' She nodded, emphasising the words. 'I'm working on it. I'd adore living here, and it would get him away from the rat-race—and all the other pressures. He's gone down terribly these last few weeks.' She spoke of him as if he were a horse.

Lindsay returned with the liqueurs and Miss Pink observed him covertly. He was a hirsute man with dark shadowed cheeks and long sideboards tinged with grey. His hair was thinning, leaving him with a grizzled tonsure which was oddly monkish, but there was nothing serene about him, on the contrary, his mood fluctuated violently between preoccupation, and nervousness when addressed. He made no effort to contribute to the conversation. Could his abstraction be due to physical pain? Miss Pink watched his eyes and hands. There was no sign of spasms and his forehead was dry. She realised that Betty Lindsay had asked a question.

'I'm sorry; I didn't catch that.'

'What are you hoping to do tomorrow?'

'I'm going out with the young man from Largo: Colin Irwin.'

'Good Lord! When did you meet him?' Miss Pink smiled gently and the other was flustered. 'I do apologise; I mean, did you know him before your arrival? You must have done.'

'In a way. I brought him over from the mainland. We met at the Kyle.'

'I see.' Betty stared at her with unintentional rudeness. Her husband asked, surprisingly in view of his former silence: 'What did he tell you?'

Miss Pink leaned back in her chair while they watched her intently. 'Of course,' she murmured, 'he never stopped talking. He talked about Skye, birds, crofters....'

'He's a great gossip,' Betty said.

'You've been out with him?'

'Oh no.' The denial was prudish. 'He's not a certificated guide.'

'Yes.'

'You don't mind that?' Lindsay asked roughly.

Miss Pink, who was sitting so that she half faced the door to the hall, caught a movement outside, and although she made some vague remark about judging Irwin when she saw him on the hill, her attention was focused on the two strangers who appeared in the doorway.

They were an ill-assorted pair: an exquisitely beautiful girl, glowing with youth and health, and a much older man: heavy, florid, without grace. He wore jeans and a light polo-necked jumper which was too small for him. He looked as if he'd dressed deliberately for the bar and this was the best he could manage. On the other hand, the girl wore a startling lilac frock, vaguely Regency with a high waist and draped skirt. Against an impression of mauve cobwebs her arms and shoulders— and much of her breasts—glowed gold.

She stood at the bar and waited, her glorious eyes following her companion who came across the room to Miss Pink's table, put a large hand possessively on Lindsay's shoulder, leered at Betty and, ignoring Miss Pink, said loudly: 'Who's in the chair then?'

Lindsay started up with an exclamation, his eyes alight with pleasure and his words tumbling over each other.

'No, let me ... You're late ... What on earth are you *wearing*? What'll it be? Glenmorangie?'

They were turning away when Betty called loudly: 'George!'

The men glanced over their shoulders. Betty looked at Miss Pink.

'This is George Watkins, who's guiding us,' she said firmly. 'George, this is Miss Pink, who you'll have heard of—'

He sketched a nod. 'How do,' he flung at her and moved after Lindsay.

Betty smiled ruefully. 'A bit of a peasant, our George—and he's the first one to admit it. A rough diamond though. We like him.'

'His friend is very attractive,' Miss Pink said.

The two men approached the bar where Gordon Hamlyn stood rigidly, his astonished eyes still on the girl who, without any sign of awkwardness, was waiting for someone else to make a move. That one is used to waiting, Miss Pink thought with strong disapproval.

Ken Maynard and his wife, in easy chairs by the door, were talking urgently—at least, Maynard was urgent, his wife cool, but whatever she said was delivered incisively. Her eyes glittered and she lit one cigarette from the stub of the last. Then Maynard rose and spoke to the girl who looked at him levelly, smiled, and moved a step closer to George Watkins.

'She's pretty,' Betty remarked, as if arriving at an independent opinion.

Since Miss Pink could think of nothing to say that was neither indelicate nor critical, she thought it better to say nothing.

Expressionlessly, not looking at her face, Hamlyn placed a drink in front of the girl. It looked like lemonade. He had already served the men. Lindsay paid, talking the while with animation to Watkins. Miss Pink had the guide in profile and observed that he regarded his client with supercilious amusement but perhaps that was his habitual expression. There was a twist to the lips that could have been a sneer, and a lift of one eyebrow, obvious when he turned full-face to the mirror behind the bar. He was vain, too.

Maynard bought drinks, exchanged a word with Hamlyn, and went back to his wife leaving the girl standing behind Watkins' large back, looking ornamental but a trifle forlorn. Miss Pink caught her eye after a moment and moved her lips. The girl came across the room obediently.

'Sit here,' Miss Pink commanded. 'You'll be tired after your long walk.'

She glanced at the bar then sat down, holding her glass in both hands like a talisman. Miss Pink introduced herself and Betty and learned that the girl was called Terry Cooke.

'Are you staying in Glen Shira long?' Betty asked.

'I don't know how long my friend is staying.' She hesitated. 'Is it you he's climbing with?'

'That's right; we've got another week.'

'I think he means to go home when you go.' She wrinkled her forehead. 'Well, I'll have had a week here. It was worth coming.' She didn't sound convinced.

Betty asked harshly, 'Do you go everywhere with him?'

The girl was surprised. 'Not everywhere. He came up here on his own, and I wouldn't have come but I got the sack and there was nothing else to do. I shouldn't have come all the same.' Her voice dropped.

'Why not?' There was no joviality about Betty now; she was sharp as a razor.

'He's got his work.'

'He has his evenings free; he gets down about six o'clock. You'll have all next week with him.'

'Yes.' It was a whisper. The lovely eyes were agonised.

'He's a moody chap,' Betty said with relish and then looked embarrassed as Miss Pink turned bland eyes on her.

'You can say that again,' Terry murmured.

Vera Hamlyn entered the room from the hall. She'd changed into a short linen dress and had the air of an off-duty member of the staff rather than one on terms of equality with the guests. The distinction was subtle but Miss Pink sensed some embarrassment in the atmosphere. Vera carried a glass and, crossing to the window, said apologetically, 'You don't mind if I join you?' and drew up a chair as she spoke. Hamlyn was a caricature of amazement, confirming Miss Pink's impression that his wife's appearance this side of the bar was not a common occurrence.

'You must be George's friend,' Vera said, and the girl smiled wanly. 'How long are you staying?'

'Only a week.'

Vera nodded. 'What are you going to do?'

'I haven't thought about it. Sunbathe, go for walks....'

'How nice for George.' Vera appeared abstracted and Miss Pink stirred. Terry shrugged and looked sullen.

'He *did* know you were coming?' Betty asked. 'He never said a word to us.'

'He didn't know.'

'Oh dear.' Vera's tone was full of sympathy. 'What will you do?'

'What *can* I do?'

Vera glanced at Betty. 'You might go to Portree,' she told the girl. 'There are always vacancies in the hotels and they'd fall over themselves to engage you. Can you do bar work?'

'I've done it,' Terry said listlessly, then, with more spirit, glancing towards Hamlyn: 'Would you take me for a week?'

'No.' The tone was flat. 'We don't need staff.' More pleasantly: 'The Royal is always short-handed, and then there are places in Broadford, and a very big hotel at the Kyle—'

Betty said, 'There's work all over the islands and on the mainland if you're prepared to put your back into it; you could have your pick of jobs.'

'I suppose so. I could go back to London if it comes to that. I'm more used to working in boutiques.'

'They don't go in for boutiques on Skye,' Betty said coldly. 'It's different from London here—and there's absolutely nothing to do in the evenings.'

'I don't want much.'

Vera said acidly, 'You've got to have money for clothes and food; you've got to do *some* work, or do you live on social security?'

'Not all of the time.' She wasn't affronted. 'But I get most of my clothes given me, food as well a lot of the time. You don't need much money really. People eat too much.'

'Of course, if you *beg*—' Betty's voice shook with anger, '—you don't need much, and then you'll always be able to get the price of a meal out of a man.'

It went clean over her head. 'Chaps don't give me money so

36

much; they usually give me a meal, in a restaurant like—or a caff if they're lorry drivers.'

Her voice carried. Maynard was listening, his eyes shining with delight, but Lavender was sober and intent, straining her ears.

'Have you any family?' Miss Pink asked equably.

'I haven't got a father. And my mum's married to a bloke I —don't get on with, so I don't go home.'

'When did you leave school?'

She grinned for the first time. 'When did I ever go to school? Officially I left this year, in July.'

'Should you be drinking?' Vera asked. It seemed the epitome of an anti-climax.

'I don't drink.'

Everyone stared at her tumbler and noted the bubbles rising in her lemonade.

'Tomorrow's Sunday,' Vera went on, recovering quickly. 'You can't make a move till Monday. I suggest you have a lazy day on the shore while George is climbing and you can spend the evening with him because the bar isn't open to non-residents on Sunday. We're not open to the public at any time in fact; George is allowed in because he's Mrs Lindsay's guide, as a special favour. Then on Monday you can go to Portree and look for work, although you're more likely to find a suitable job on the mainland. Inverness is a very nice place and there's a lot happening there. They have boutiques too.'

'London would be better.' Betty's tone was pregnant with meaning.

'You're right,' Terry said, and sighed. 'It's not really my scene, is it?' She glanced over her shoulder at George Watkins who hadn't looked at her since they entered the room. 'I'll give it till Monday,' she said hopefully.

Madge Fraser came in. Her casual gaze went round the room, observing the occupants without surprise until it rested on Terry Cooke. The others watched her, the Maynards like alert pointers. Only Watkins and Lindsay, after glances which were no more than acknowledgement of her entrance, ignored her.

Hamlyn looked a query, received a nod, and drew her a whisky which she brought over to the table in the window.

'You're George's friend,' she remarked without preamble and in the cool tone girls used to each other.

'I've known him a while.'

'Staying long?'

The other stiffened. 'It depends.'

'On George?'

'What's it got to do with you?'

Madge took a sip of her whisky. 'Nothing.'

Suddenly Terry addressed Miss Pink. 'Do you think I'd find work in Portree?'

'I think you would be happier in London.'

Miss Pink did not mean happier because, she thought, no one could be happier in London than on Skye, but she didn't want the girl to look for work in Portree or even the Kyle of Lochalsh. Not happier—

'What kind of work are you looking for?' Madge regarded the lilac frock and its *décolletage* incuriously.

Terry said, 'I'm easy.'

'You could get a job anywhere.'

'What do you mean by that?'

'Hell, with your looks?'

The girl seemed puzzled by the reactions she aroused at this table. She would be used to attention but not, perhaps, quite so much. And she was surrounded by women.

'You're wasted here, my dear.' Miss Pink's voice was kind. 'Has no one offered you the kind of work where you could use your appearance: films perhaps, or television?'

'People have, but they never meant it.'

'You want an agent,' Madge said. 'A chap who cares about you; not the kind that doesn't think any farther than jumping into bed. A queer would do nicely. Why don't you go back to town and find the best television agent who's a homosexual? Can you act?'

'You're not serious?'

'Christ! Do you expect everyone to take advantage of you?'

Miss Pink was speculative behind the thick spectacles. She did not think it would be easy to exploit Terry. Because she was infatuated by the oaf at the bar, that didn't mean her behaviour was usual. It could be one of those instances of an attractive and otherwise balanced woman falling—just once in her life—for a rogue. It happened even to mature women, women with judgement, although, of course, judgement failed in the one direction. But how much judgement did this child have in any direction? Safer. That was what she'd been thinking: Terry would be, not happier in London than on the island, but safer.

Chapter 4

'I'M SORRY,' Colin Irwin said, 'I can't come with you after all.'

Miss Pink regarded him thoughtfully. It was ten o'clock on the Sunday morning and, having waited in vain for him to come to Glen Shira House, having seen him fetching water from the burn at eight o'clock, she'd walked across to Largo to find out what was keeping him.

'The fact is,' he went on uncomfortably, 'I've got a visitor.'

Playing for time, she turned and studied Sgurr Alasdair. Irwin was biting his lip; he may have been up at eight but at close quarters he looked tired and worried. There was also an air of defiance about him.

Miss Pink said: 'I'm sure you wouldn't break a previous engagement without good reason ...'

She left it hanging and made to move away; he hadn't asked her in. They descended a rough slope to the river where there were so many boulders exposed that one could cross anywhere. On the other side, the colonel's woodland came right down to the bank.

Irwin said with suppressed fury: 'A girl came here last night. I was reading late and she saw my lamp. Some lout had knocked her about and thrown her out of his tent. So I took her in. She's in a bit of a state and I'd rather not leave her.'

'What's her name?'

'Terry. She didn't tell me her surname.'

'It's Cooke. She was in the hotel last night with George Watkins. It was he, of course—? I think it's an excellent idea for you to spend a day with her. Is there anything to be done or will she recover with rest—and security?'

'The worst of it is,' he began, not answering her but following his own line of thought, 'she seems used to it. She's not upset about the violence, but the fact that he threw her out— I mean, that he doesn't *want* her! Can you understand that?'

'It happens. It's deplorable, but even the nicest girls do come under the spell of thugs: bewitched rather than falling in love. Strange—' her eyes followed the flight of a raven towards the shore, '—how people who are not quite so strong as they might be, and immature ones easily fall prey to bad influences where they resist the good.' She looked at him candidly. 'Perhaps they're less resistant to good influences after a nasty shock,' she suggested. 'You stay with her; don't leave her on her own to-day. Watkins has gone out—but she might brood on her own.'

He still looked anxious. 'I've to go to Sligachan tomorrow for two days. It means leaving her on her own in the cottage.'

'See how today goes,' Miss Pink urged. 'If she doesn't—'

His eyes sharpened at something behind her. She turned and saw Terry Cooke in the doorway of the cottage, still wearing her lilac dress. Miss Pink pondered for a moment, then climbed the bank again, Irwin following. Terry watched her approach without expression but when the girl looked at Irwin her eyes softened. Her lip was swollen and split and one eye was partly closed and bruised black. Both arms were grazed as if she'd fallen heavily when running. The dress was in tatters.

'You go out with this lady,' she told Irwin, 'I don't mind.'

He must have told her he'd intended to guide Miss Pink today. The latter said cheerfully, brooking no argument: 'I changed my mind.' Then, practically, 'Have you left anything in Watkins' tent?'

Terry looked at Irwin. 'Your gear,' he explained. He turned to Miss Pink. 'She did. I'll go across for it.'

They all went, Terry barefooted and limping a little.

The river ran into the sea at the side of the glen, leaving half a mile of unbroken sand stretching to the far side of the valley.

Above the shore were grassy dunes and the camp site which was best reached from Largo by a swing bridge a short distance downstream. The MacNeills' farm, Rahane, was the only other dwelling on this side of the river. It stood close to the tide-line on the miniature estuary.

They crossed the bridge upstream of a ford and climbed the bank through broom bushes to a track which led to the camp. Terry guided them to an old Ford van and an orange tent. Miss Pink unzipped the latter and exposed a chaos of squalor. With some show of eagerness (she must have thought she'd seen the last of them), Terry retrieved her possessions.

'How much money did you have?' Miss Pink asked as the girl backed out of the entrance with a green suède shoulder bag.

Irwin said quickly, 'She doesn't need money; I've got plenty.'

'Have a look.' Miss Pink indicated the bag.

He lifted the flap and took out a leather purse, opened it, shook it. It was empty.

'How much?' Miss Pink pressed.

'There wasn't a pound,' Terry said, almost in tears. 'It's not worth bothering about.'

'Of course it isn't,' Miss Pink agreed suddenly. 'Forget about it. Have you got everything? Now you'd better go home and have some breakfast.' Across the mouth of the river some cows were gathered about Rahane. 'If we're lucky,' she went on, with unconscious irony considering the late hour, 'the MacNeills will have milked. Go and get a dozen eggs, Mr Irwin, and plenty of milk.'

She gave him a pound note and at the bridge he strode away to the farm while the women strolled towards Largo. Miss Pink glanced back at the dunes. There were only a few tents on the camp site besides that of Watkins, and one camping van. People had been moving about the site but they'd paid no attention to the elderly woman and the girl in the ragged dress. She wondered how bizarre a situation would have to be before their attention was engaged.

'You didn't think of asking for help from any of those people last night?' she asked. Largo was some distance from the camp site.

'I met Colin last evening when I went over to Rahane for the milk.' With her bad foot, Miss Pink thought grimly. 'Besides,' the girl went on shame-facedly, gesturing to the dunes, 'all these people are couples, or with kids. And Colin was the only one with a light. It was late, see, when we got back.' Her voice dropped. 'I ran away from him—from George—and when I stopped and looked, there was the light, quite close. I fell over the stones in the river; that's how this happened, I guess.' She held out her arms.

Miss Pink had been the first to go to bed last night. She'd wondered at the time what would be the outcome when Watkins decided to leave the hotel. He was not the kind of man who would go home sober. As they walked slowly back to Largo she reflected that, taking everything into consideration, the girl had been lucky.

She left them absorbed in cooking and each other and walked back past the big house and through the wood to take the main path that climbed straight out of the glen towards the Cuillin. She was preoccupied—which is not a bad thing on long upward gradients—and she plodded on for twenty minutes only half aware of the sun on her damp face, and moorland smells: peat and heather and baking rock. Grasshoppers rasped, and from the glen came the whine of a tractor.

Suddenly she stopped, appalled. Her vision had been confined to dry earth and heather stalks about her boots; now the land stopped, dropped away, and for a moment there was only a green abyss below. She was on the lip of the ravine which contained the burn emerging from Coire na Banachdich and the greenery was the tops of silver birches which, on the near side of the depression, plunged so steeply that one wondered where and how their roots found purchase. On the far side, the ground was even steeper with vertical rock walls where, in the sheltered and humid environment, every ledge and scoop was a riot of vegetation. In the back of this sculpted amphitheatre the

43

cliffs were over a hundred feet high and the burn poured over the lip in the waterfall called Eas Mor.

Today the fall was a broken thread, still impressive because of its height but nothing like so sensational as it was when in spate.

She moved back to the path, and the sound of water faded to be replaced by the hum of insects and the whine of the tractor. After a while she heard a distant but unmistakably metallic clatter and realised that the tractor had stopped. She looked back towards the settlement.

Largo and Rahane were full in the sunshine. The sound of the tractor's engine came to her again and she pulled the binoculars from her rucksack to focus on the farm. After a few moments she discovered the tractor moving along a level green shelf towards the buildings. It was drawing no implement but a hydraulic shovel was attached to its front. She worked backwards, along the shelf to its termination at a gully in the sea cliffs. There, as she'd suspected (for the clatter could have been only something large falling a long distance), was Rahane's rubbish tip: at the back of the once beautiful inlet called Scarf Geo.

She put the binoculars away and turned towards the mountains. If anything could be done to stop crofters throwing their waste, from old cars to drums which had contained toxic chemicals, over the nearest cliff, it could not be done at this moment. Now, seven hours of the ridge lay ahead and, like an efficient detective, she turned, metaphorically and literally, from Scarf Geo and, looking southwards, concentrated on the islands and the nearer moors where water gleamed in the peat and once, long ago, she had found black-throated divers nesting.

The path meandered through dried-out bogs, skirted a lochan, climbed steeply to turn the corner where the world of wide seas and skies shrank suddenly to a narrow corrie hemmed by cliffs. But the impression of claustrophobia was momentary for the eye was drawn upwards to a skyline of gaps and towers and pinnacles while, across the mouth of the corrie, stood the Sron: Sron na Ciche, a concave precipice of dark rock where the

44

coloured specks that were climbers looked terribly lonely and vulnerable. The Lindsays and Watkins were here. Madge and Maynard were round in the next corrie.

The cliff was a place for companions and a rope. Miss Pink made her way to the back of the corrie and the innocuous pleasures of Sgurr Sgumain with its more broken face.

Again her preoccupation showed, this time in her making a false start. She failed to notice that the loose and steepening rock up which she was scrambling bore no traces of previous climbers. It wasn't until she was brought up short by an impending wall where chimneys were wet even in the drought that she realised her mistake but, unwilling to retreat down something which, from the top, assumed a much higher angle than had been apparent from below, she wandered under the wall trying in vain to find a way through.

At some risk she negotiated rising basalt dykes which stood proud above the basic rock, but it wasn't until she was descending an enormous balloon of black lichen like a tumour on the face that she came to her senses.

She descended carefully, to find the correct line farther along: cleaned of lichen and the rock smoothed by nailed boots. In half an hour she reached the crest and looked over to see the Sron, with figures, much closer, and more human in scale. A thousand feet below, the peacock eye of a lochan was winking in the sun.

She came to the final tower of Sgumain and turned it by a trod like a chamois track which brought her at last to the main ridge. Across Glen Sligachan rose the Red Hills and beyond them and just distinguishable through the haze, the great sea lochs of the Inner Sound penetrated the hinterland of Knoydart and Applecross. Then gently, and so quiet she could hear the air in its pinions, an eagle drifted past, and before it vanished round a near buttress, she saw the wings come up and the feathered talons brake and knew it was going to land.

She scrambled after it, forcing herself to go carefully because there was a drop into Coir' a' Ghrunnda and if she slipped she might not stop for several hundred feet, but as she rounded the

45

buttress and thought there was a small pinnacle perched on the edge, she saw its eye. She had one glimpse of the fierce profile then the wings spread and, dropping a little under its own weight, it sailed down the corrie leaving her breathless with pleasure.

In a dream she returned and, still below the crest, heard familiar voices. She stopped, saw a party climbing along the ridge and heard George Watkins say: 'I haven't got all bloody day to hang around pulling you up; you go round the side and up the chimney.'

Miss Pink wore drab colours and she was in shadow. She sat down in a corner and watched the Lindsays climbing carefully behind their guide towards what climbers called the Bad Step. The clients carried rucksacks but Watkins was unencumbered except for a rope. Betty Lindsay had the second rope.

The acoustics were in Miss Pink's favour. She heard Betty Lindsay say clearly: 'There's plenty of time. Really, George, if you're so concerned at getting down for opening time—'

Lindsay said, 'Oh, come off it; stop needling him!'

'*Me* needling *him!* He's been getting at me all day—'

'Shut up!' Watkins was standing below the Bad Step, uncoiling the rope. He hesitated, then handed the end to Betty without looking at her, and turned to the rock. Unsecured, Betty pulled out a few coils deftly so that the rope wouldn't snag as he stepped up the broken wall. It was only a few moves but there was a nasty drop underneath. Watkins' climbing was clumsy and, although he got up, he was not a pleasure to watch. He belayed at the top and took in the slack. Betty tied on casually and waited. Her pack looked enormous.

'Come on,' Watkins said.

She stepped off the ground and went up the wall with astonishing neatness considering her build and her load. As she drew level with Watkins she must have said something because he exclaimed, 'Christ! You think I'd trust him to you? Take that rope off and get out of the bloody way!'

She untied and moved on a few yards to sit down and watch. Miss Pink took the binoculars out of her sack and raised them carefully. Adjusting the range, the other woman's face was in startling close-up: flushed from the sun and the constriction of her helmet certainly, but not appearing in the least put out by the outrageous behaviour of the guide.

Lindsay was making a hash of the Bad Step. The secret was knowing where the fingerholds were, for the rock overhung slightly and the footholds sloped. Miss Pink suspected that, far from being the kind of man who was encouraged when others encountered no difficulty, the reverse was the case here. His standard was far below that of his wife.

A steady murmur of encouragement came from the guide, punctuated by complaints from Lindsay. The man was tired and inclining to panic.

'All right then,' he cried suddenly on a rising note. 'If I come off—you've got me?'

'Sure.' Watkins was chuckling. 'Come on then: up you come!'

Watkins braced himself for a fall but with a wild heave and a grab Lindsay was up. There were exclamations of relief and congratulation from Betty, and Watkins was laughing loudly. They milled a little, the rope was coiled and, still oblivious of the watcher, the party moved away towards the summit.

Miss Pink replaced the binoculars and fastened the strap of her pack. Her eyes wandered over the ridges and down to the corrie underneath where a little brown and green lochan shone in the sun and two remote figures made splashes close to the shore. She smiled. That was more pleasant than the scene she had just witnessed.

After a while the bathers came out of the water and they were so consistently pale in that well of boulder fields that they must be naked. Miss Pink was in the act of rising when she paused and took another look at them. *Two* climbers—and Maynard and Madge were in that corrie.... She shrugged. In her own youth she had often swum in mountain lakes with male climbers but—and she pursed her lips in disapproval—none of them had a wife like Lavender.

'How long has MacNeill been tipping down Scarf Geo?'

47

Behind the bar Hamlyn turned slowly to face Miss Pink. 'Two years.' His eyes were furious.

'We had the same trouble in Wales when I lived there.' She spoke with sympathy. 'I haven't come across it in Cornwall—yet.'

'The English are civilised. Here they've hardly advanced since the Dark Ages.' He warmed to the theme. 'Timothy Barker was here in May: the anthropologist. He was explaining the development of civilisation—domestically, that is. You start with a house of sorts, which is nothing more than a shelter from the elements; that's subsistence level. But once cultivators have a surplus, first they build up stock and implements, then domestic appliances: pots, pans, a better cooking range; nowadays it's deep freezers and spin dryers, of course—bought by women whose mothers took in washing! And after necessities, or what *they* think of as necessities, they start to ornament their houses: plastic flowers, china Alsatians on the window sill, coloured bathroom suites. They've gone past the stage of keeping the coal in the bath and they don't throw their rubbish out of the back door any longer. No, they take it to the edge of their land and tip it over a cliff.'

Miss Pink's shoulders slumped but she tried again.

'Doesn't the Council collect rubbish from the glen?'

'Of course it does. But the lorry can't cross to Rahane; there's only the footbridge. The ford is negotiable for the tractor, and young MacNeill even takes the cattle wagon across, but the Council lorry won't risk getting bogged down and asking the MacNeills to pull it out with the tractor, so Rahane's meant to take their rubbish across to the camp site in bags. They're too bone idle for that.'

There were footsteps on the gravel outside the front door, and voices.

'Ah, Miss Pink!' Betty Lindsay came in, hot and jolly, 'Where did you go?'

She murmured something about Sgumain, and Lindsay and Watkins shouldered into the room, a little larger than life, like all parties just down off the hill. Miss Pink had come in half an

48

hour ago and had already bathed and changed.

'We'll have a pint of draught lager each,' Watkins ordered. 'Off the ice.'

Hamlyn stared at him without moving.

'Please,' Watkins added, and grinned sheepishly.

Hamlyn drew the lager with obvious reluctance. The Lindsays' faces were carefully expressionless.

Lavender entered with a swirl of skirts. She was in orange tonight and smelt of musky scent. She started to talk to Miss Pink intimately, as if they were old acquaintances. Madge and Maynard appeared in the hall, seeming subdued after the impact of the first party. As Madge came to the bar Betty asked: 'Did you do the White Slab?'

'Yes.'

'Then what?'

'Nothing else,' Maynard put in, following his guide, smiling at Miss Pink. 'It was too hot. Good evening, dear,' to his wife.

Watkins said, with a nasty gleam in his eye: 'That was you swimming, in Coir' a' Ghrunnda.'

'That's right.' Madge took a whisky from Hamlyn. 'What did you do?' she asked Lindsay.

Lavender had gone rigid. For the second time in twenty-four hours, Miss Pink walked across the room and sought solace in the vista of the Cuillin.

After dinner she joined Betty and Madge at the table in the window.

'Was anything said about Terry today?' she asked of Betty.

'Why, yes.' The other paused, then said confidentially, 'She's been an awful nuisance. In fact, she's cleared off.'

Madge looked at Betty but said nothing. Miss Pink said, 'He beat her up badly last night and she took refuge with Colin Irwin.'

Betty stirred uneasily. 'Well, that's her story. He did tell us she'd shacked up with Irwin, but as for beating her up: when they got back to the tent it was she who attacked *him*. He had to throw her out to protect himself.'

'Have you seen her?'

'No, and I don't want to. I know her type.'

'Have *you* seen her?' Madge asked Miss Pink with interest. 'Yes.'

'George always knocks his women about; he'd be hard put to it to find one more stupid than himself and he resents anyone who's more intelligent.' She considered her own words. 'He kicks the rock when he can't get up a climb,' she added.

Betty, who had been smouldering during the first part of this, was suddenly deflated. 'That kicking business,' she said earnestly. 'He's so furious with himself.'

'I know.' Madge agreed with the obvious. 'He's immature.' She turned to Miss Pink. 'So what will Terry do now?'

'I hope she'll stay with Irwin, at least for long enough for him to try to instil some values into her.'

'She'd be all right with Colin,' Madge agreed.

'The trouble is,' Miss Pink said, looking at Betty, 'Irwin's going to Sligachan for two days.'

The other frowned but it was Madge who responded. 'George isn't going to go across to Largo while Colin's away. I mean, if he's thrown her out, he doesn't want her. He's not neurotic, you know. I expect she got too much for him.'

'Just what do you mean by that?' Betty was belligerent.

'She's too sexy.'

'Do you think that's all George wants?'

'You weren't listening; I was saying the opposite. He doesn't want it.'

'Oh, you're impossible!'

Betty got up quickly and flung out of the room.

'Got her on the raw,' Madge remarked. 'Silly woman. Nice climber though.'

'Do you always say what comes into your mind?' Miss Pink asked, between awe and amusement.

Madge gave a little snort of appreciation. 'Why not? I've got my hands full just living—or rather, making a living. I can't be bothered to think as well.'

'Like Terry,' Miss Pink murmured.

'Not quite.' The guide was dry. 'She's not making a living—poor kid.'

'Why "poor kid"?'

'Well, she's cut out for trouble, isn't she?'

'Not necessarily. I think she'll make a go of it with young Irwin.' Miss Pink looked at the other defiantly but surprised at herself for getting worked up about this.

Madge grinned. 'You've got to keep that kind on a collar and chain. I don't give much for Colin's chances if he's going to leave her for two days after only just meeting her.'

Chapter 5

HER GLIMPSES OF the Sron had unsettled Miss Pink and although a scramble along the crest of the Cuillin was great fun, she knew that she would be even happier were she to reach the top by way of a rock climb. Maynard perceived this and before she went to bed an invitation to climb tomorrow had been made and accepted.

So the following morning they tramped up Coire na Banachdich and climbed the easy Window Buttress of Sgurr Dearg— a puzzling choice for it was a short route on the side of the mountain, but one which was explained when they were lunching on the summit under the Inaccessible Pinnacle. Maynard said diffidently: 'Madge wants to do the South Crack; would you care to have a go?' Miss Pink glanced at the expressionless guide and knew that it was the client who had set his heart on the route.

'I have a dim memory of something overhanging for a hundred feet,' she countered cautiously.

'The pinnacle leans back,' Madge told her. 'It's nearer seventy feet than a hundred and it's got holds.'

'I'll watch you first.'

'Watch me,' Maynard said ruefully. 'That's more to the point.'

It was an interesting performance and it possessed a significance which she was to remember afterwards. There was a casual intimacy between the climbers which was intriguing because it was more the activity to which the intimacy referred, rather than an emotional relationship.

Although Madge was obviously the superior they worked as a team and Miss Pink realised that the guide had an unexpected grace. It was evident from her familiarity with the holds that she could have climbed the route solo, yet as she placed her slings, clipped in her rope and, watching it fall, caught her second's eye—throughout balanced on small holds above a deepening drop—she had the air of accepting the man as an integral part of this delicate machine. There was a mutual illusion of dependence, but on her part, assumed. It put a gloss on her ability.

Maynard followed, struggling a little, his breathing audible to the watcher on the ground. Then she tied on and, with a sinking stomach, stepped into the crack.

It was not so steep as she'd imagined, and all the holds were there so long as she didn't panic and miss them. Like Maynard, she had trouble with a bulge at thirty feet where she was forced to leave the spurious security of the crack and emerge on the smooth wall but otherwise the climb was a matter of striking a balance between the need to proceed slowly enough that she had time to find the next hold, yet not so slow that her strength gave out. She reached the top exhausted, trembling, and glowing with achievement.

Madge continued to surprise her. When Maynard was taking photographs of hazy depths framed between gully walls, and trying to find the right filter to bring out the inkiness of Loch Coruisk against its sunlit shore, Miss Pink voiced her trepidation. He was like a heedless child, scrambling one-handed above the tremendous drops.

'He won't hurt,' Madge chided. 'You worry too much.' She caught the other's glance and smiled. 'You can't worry in this job.'

'What about your responsibility?'

'Don't know if it's ever been defined, as to limits. So far as I'm concerned, when the client's off the rope, providing he's adult, he's responsible, not I. Can you imagine me, now, calling across to him not to get too near the edge? How many clients would I keep that way?'

53

'You might save some.'

'If they're that daft, they can be spared.'

'You're a hard woman, Madge.'

The other sighed. 'You thought that last night. *That* was because of Terry getting into trouble.' She turned candid eyes on Miss Pink. 'So she gets knocked about by fellows and will have two or three kids before she's twenty: what can you do about it? Why waste your energy on her?'

'You seem to be looking at it from a biological point of view: basically, survival of the fittest. But on that basis, she's definitely worth helping because of her beauty and her health.'

'That's nothing. She's got no brain.'

'Oh come! Just because she was infatuated with Watkins! She's learned her lesson.'

'Rubbish. She'll be bored with Colin within the week and she'll go back to George or, if he won't have her, to another guy who'll knock her about. She's made for it—like battered wives. Surely you've come across those?'

Miss Pink nodded sadly. 'But it's her youth; that's what's so shocking.'

'Well, her *age*,' Madge demurred. 'She's experienced enough.'

'Hardly.' The tone was firm. 'She may have had more sexual adventures than many mature women but she's too young to have learned anything from them. That's her tragedy.'

'But not mine.' The guide's face was set and surprisingly angry. She stood up. 'I have to look for a cache.'

'A what?'

'A place to hide some food. I'm going to do the ridge when I can get a couple of days to myself.'

The whole range: seven miles long, with twenty peaks, was a test of endurance for mountaineers. Miss Pink accompanied the guide like an interested terrier, peering with her into holes under rocks, sniffing out a place that would be recognisable in mist. Some distance away was a tall rock shaped like a man and rather larger.

'That stands out in cloud,' Madge observed. 'I always mistake it for a person.'

54

They scrambled across to this bollard and found a place where food might be cached under a slab about six feet from its base.

'If I roll a stone against the opening, no one will know anything's inside.'

'Would climbers steal food?'

'They'd take anything. Some of them live by stealing.' She seemed to have recovered her spirits.

They descended to Glen Shira by way of the splendid head-wall of Coire na Banachdich: a place where Miss Pink had never been before, and when they reached the floor of the corrie and looked back, she was awe-struck.

'How did we come down? It's all rock. I never realised we were on such a wall.'

'You only see the walls looking up,' Madge reminded her. 'We zig-zagged down the ledges.'

'She knows the way,' Maynard said. 'She can do it in cloud —and in the dark.'

'Anyone can,' Madge pointed out. 'It's only a matter of experience—' She grinned at Miss Pink.

'Of knowledge,' Maynard corrected. 'Not necessarily of this ground, but of any mountain terrain. It's also a matter of knowing one's limits, and after that: concentration, keeping your cool. A guide doesn't panic, right?'

Madge shrugged, too sure of herself to be embarrassed.

'You're never worried?' Miss Pink asked casually as they turned to the glen.

'No, not really.' She thought for a moment. 'Not up here.'

Miss Pink entered her room and crossed to the window. Largo's door was open and a naked figure lay on the grass in front of the cottage. A man was approaching from the direction of Rahane. As Miss Pink watched, he stopped, the sunbather sat up, then rose and went indoors. The visitor could be Willie MacNeill.

Terry emerged wearing jeans and some kind of pink top. The

man approached now and the two of them went inside the cottage. Miss Pink thought the whole episode was an amusing display of etiquette.

She ran her bath. After a few minutes she noticed that Largo's chimney was smoking thickly.

She went down to the cocktail lounge to find all the residents assembled. Lavender tried to corner her and draw her out on the events of the day. Who had climbed with whom? When Miss Pink had made it plain that they had all been on one rope, she was pressed as to the order in which they'd climbed. She found Lavender's obsessive jealousy tiresome, and eventually managed to address herself to Hamlyn, demanding details from him of the Cuillin traverse. But he failed to come to her assistance; on the contrary, he added fuel to Lavender's fire by mention of 'constricted stances' and laboured jokes on the embarrassing situations which resulted when strangers of mixed sex were in close proximity above big drops. Lavender plucked restlessly at her neck.

Miss Pink moved to join the Lindsays, who stopped talking at her approach. Betty said, on a high false note: 'We were wondering how long the heat wave would last.'

Andrew Lindsay went to the bar.

'Poor love.' His wife's glance followed him and her eyes were shifty. 'His ulcer's bothering him.'

Miss Pink commiserated and wondered what was wrong. He was drinking double whiskies: strange treatment for an ulcer. Maynard, who had been looking out of the window with Madge, came across and asked if Miss Pink would accompany them to Sgurr nan Gillean the following day. She declined, not wanting to confine them to her own standard. To her mind, the South Crack had been a flash in the pan.

Madge said idly, 'I wonder what Colin did today? There's nothing hard to do at that end.'

'Such arrogance,' Maynard reproved. '*Everything* is hard on the Cuillin.'

Betty caught Miss Pink's eye and remarked ambiguously, 'So she'll be alone tonight.'

56

Madge turned from the window. 'I might pop over there this evening.'

Her words were clear in a sudden silence and Lavender said spitefully, 'You do that; you can compare notes.'

Maynard walked out of the room.

'It must be nearly feeding time,' Betty said, and gave an inane giggle.

Madge stared at Lavender as the other woman lit a cigarette. Miss Pink asked with simulated interest, 'Are you out to break the record for the traverse of the ridge?'

Madge gave a deep sigh and turned blank eyes on the questioner. 'No.' She opened her hands and stared at the palms, then turned them over and clenched the fingers tightly. She spoke like a somnambulist. 'I'm fit; I want to stretch myself.' She grinned emptily at Miss Pink. 'That's it,' she said brightly, 'it's getting my teeth into something, you know? One gets bored with routine.' She yawned, raising her hand to her mouth belatedly, her eyes on Lavender. ''Times I get sick of people.'

During the evening the residents disappeared. Over dinner an intense conversation between the Lindsays developed into an argument which led to a quarrel with Lindsay walking angrily out of the dining room and Betty hurrying after him. They were halfway through the pudding and didn't return.

The Maynards didn't go to the lounge for coffee and Miss Pink and Madge were left to themselves. Even the guide stayed only long enough for politeness' sake and then excused herself. Miss Pink remembered that the other had said she might go to Largo. Reflecting that Watkins could put in an appearance at any moment, she said goodnight to Hamlyn and went upstairs. It was eight-thirty. There was a light in Largo. She wished she knew what Watkins was doing.

The following morning Madge and Maynard left early, and even the Lindsays' party had gone by the time Miss Pink was ready to set off for what she anticipated would be a gentle walk along the coast. She was struggling into her rucksack straps when

Colin Irwin came hurriedly across the lawn. He didn't reply to her greeting.

'Where did she go?' he asked.

Miss Pink's stomach contracted. 'Terry? She was there last night. When did you get home?'

'I just got back. The place is empty. She hasn't even left a note.'

'Has she taken her things?'

'Yes, everything.'

'She must have left either late last night—after eight-thirty when I saw her light—or this morning.'

'She didn't walk out of the glen this morning or I'd have seen her on the road. I got a couple of lifts round. What happened was that my client caught some kind of a bug; he was up most of the night. He came over to my tent this morning and cancelled today so I came straight here once I'd had some breakfast.'

'If you came back by road, you could have missed her if she walked to Sligachan across the moor.'

'She'd never have done that. It was the way she came in on Saturday and she only had sandals. She had to go bare-footed then, and she cut her foot. Besides, she was frightened of that moor; she didn't like being on her own in the hills. She didn't mind empty houses.'

Miss Pink looked at him sharply. 'I'll come across to Largo with you; we can't talk here. There might be something you've missed.... Madge Fraser meant to go over last night. If she did, Terry may have told her where she was going. Madge has gone to Sgurr nan Gillean today.'

'I know. I passed Maynard's car on the road. They waved.'

He was very unhappy. Miss Pink said, 'Terry gave no indication at all that she might be leaving while you were away?'

'None. Did she go back to Watkins?'

They stopped and stared at each other, then looked towards the camp site. Tacitly, they changed direction and walked rapidly through the trees towards the sea. She thought that if she hadn't been with him, Irwin would have run.

They found Watkins' tent closed. Irwin called: 'Terry?' in

a hopeless voice and unzipped the entrance. Inside there was only the cluttered squalor that they had found on the first occasion and no sign of the girl nor her belongings.

They walked slowly across the dunes towards Largo. At the ford they met Willie MacNeill driving the tractor with the hydraulic shovel on the front. He stopped when Irwin waved him down.

'She was there yesterday,' the young crofter shouted above the engine. 'She didna say she was leaving.'

'What time—?'

Willie throttled down. 'It was getting on: evening time, I'd say. Six-ish, closer to seven, maybe ... She was after giving me tea. ...'

Miss Pink walked on, her feet dragging in the thick sand of the track. There were little waders on the tide-line but although she had brought her rucksack, she did not feel like using her binoculars. Behind her, Willie revved the engine, and Irwin came loping after her.

'You heard that?'

She nodded. 'What's Willie doing over here?' she asked.

'There's a strike of Council workers so Rahane's emptying the camp bins; got to get rid of the rubbish quickly in this hot weather.'

The interior of the cottage was dark, and furnished only by squatters' standards. In the living room there was a small ship's stove with a flue leading into the chimney, two old car seats and a scarred wooden table. An oil lamp hung from a hook on a beam. There was a camp cooker and a canteen of billies on the window sill among a clutter of packaged foods, old newspapers and rocks. The fire was out, the billies were clean, and there appeared to be no trace of the girl.

'She's taken everything she owned?' Miss Pink pressed.

'I haven't searched, but the obvious things have gone: bedding roll, handbag, clothes. You can look.'

She explored the rest of the cottage. On the left of the front door there was a room that would have been the parlour in better days. There was a pair of easy chairs with the stuffing coming out, and a sack half full of carrots and onions.

The stairs went straight up from the front door to a tiny landing and a bedroom above each of the rooms below. These were lit by dormer windows and each contained an iron bedstead on which were palliasses made of hessian and filled with straw or chaff. A fruit crate stood beside one bed and the stump of a candle. The crate had its back to the window. Up-ended it served as a bedside table, the partition in the middle doing duty as a shelf. As she turned it round, something moved inside: a large chip of rough green marble.

She came downstairs to find Irwin lighting the cooker.

'You'll have a cup of tea?'

'Thank you. What's this?'

He took the chip, frowned momentarily, then his face cleared. 'I gave it to her. It was my best specimen. I pick them up beside the road at Drynoch.' He gestured to the window sill and she saw, what she had missed at a cursory glance, that the rocks were interesting pieces; some were fossils, most were marble, but all were inferior to the chip she had found in the bedroom. 'I was trying to think of a way to make them into jewellery,' he explained. 'I gave her that piece and she treasured it; said she'd always keep it. You see what it means? She'd never go without it. She left it deliberately to show she's coming back.'

'Oh, yes.' Miss Pink was bright. 'That could be it.'

She dreaded the moment when he realised how much simpler it would have been for the girl to write a note—but already he'd seen that his theory was too devious.

'Well,' he admitted grudgingly, 'perhaps she forgot it.' He brightened a little. 'Then she'll write and ask me to send it. Won't she?'

But as they stared at the green chip they were both wondering why she had gone.

Chapter 6

WILLIE MACNEILL, driving along the green shelf from
Rahane to Scarf Geo, prepared himself for trouble. At the end
of the track, just beyond the place where he tipped the rubbish,
a solitary figure appeared to be waiting for him. It was the lady
who had been with Colin on the camp site.

Willie had more than a passing acquaintance with elderly
mountaineers, particularly in relation to Scarf Geo, and he wondered if this one would do as the doctor did in July: stand in
his path so that he couldn't tip. He found English ladies intimidating and as he approached this one, too fast for his own
comfort but he was too proud to slacken speed, he had the
feeling she was going to be awkward, and sure enough, here
she came: advancing to the head of the gully to take up her
stand this side of the sleepers that were his marker for lowering
the shovel. His eyes widened in panic as she raised her hand,
then, deftly, like a man, made the gesture of switching off the
engine. It was that which unnerved him. He obeyed her and
waited, momentarily defeated.

'You'll have to stop tipping,' she said firmly.

He tried to grin. 'You canna stop us—and we're tipping for
the Council now anyways; they're on strike and the man at
Portree says it's a health hazard.' He reached for the ignition.

'Go back to Rahane,' Miss Pink ordered, 'and ring the
police—'

'It's no' a poliss job, mam; they won't have nothing to do with
it. The colonel, he tried—'

'—Ask to speak to the man in charge and tell him that there

is a body in Scarf Geo—' She considered for a moment and in the silence Willie heard the sea birds calling and felt sick. 'On second thoughts,' she went on, 'go to the house and ask the colonel to telephone. Tell him that I sent you.'

He swallowed. 'I havena seen it.'

She regarded him doubtfully but led the way to the place where she'd been when he saw her first. There was a fence along the top of the cliffs and here on the edge a stretcher post was cemented in the rock.

'If you get through the wire and lean out from the post, you can see.'

He looked at her suspiciously. She saw what was in his mind: a madwoman who would pick up a rock and hammer at his fingers when all his weight was on the post. She moved back a few yards and sat down.

He kicked the post, found it firm, stooped and stepped through the wire, then, still staring at her, he gripped the post and leaned out. The concern in her face infuriated him and he looked down.

At first he saw only the recent loads draping the back of the gully which dropped in two steps to the deep and narrow inlet. The tide was high and the geo almost awash below the accumulated filth. He couldn't see anything in the water that looked like a body.

'In a plastic bag,' Miss Pink said.

He sneered. 'Body of what? A dead cat?'

'A large bag; it looks somewhat like a seal.'

There *was* a big piece of plastic down there, reflecting the sun. He couldn't remember picking up a piece of plastic that size today. There was something red underneath it. And something like a foot—

Miss Pink had stood up. She said firmly, 'Come back now.'

He felt the iron under his hand, pulled back, blundered through the wire, was surprised to notice how scorched the turf was here on top of the cliffs, and walked towards the sound of her voice. He sat down, shaking, and stared at the water, his eyes shocked.

'Who is it?' he whispered.

'I don't know yet.' She was also looking out to sea.

'I was tipping on it!'

'No harm done,' she lied, and looked at him closely. 'Do you think you can drive back to the big house?'

'Ay.' He stood up. 'You said to phone the poliss?'

She repeated her instructions and he walked towards the tractor. 'MacNeill!' He turned. 'You were at Largo last night.'

He had been very pale. Now he flushed. 'I wasna!' She said nothing. 'Early on,' he muttered. 'I came away before seven.'

'You weren't there later?'

'No.'

He made to climb on the tractor but checked and stood with his back to her, his head hanging. Slowly he turned round. He looked bewildered and dangerous.

'Why are you asking?'

'She's disappeared.'

He started back aggressively but before he reached her his face changed again. He looked as if he might burst into tears.

'You're no' thinking—' he glanced towards the cliff. *'No!'* More quietly: 'It's no' her, is it?'

'We don't know yet,' she repeated. 'Did you return to Largo after seven?'

'No, no, *no!*'

He ran and leaped on the tractor, reversed, turned and sped back along the track, the shovel spilling rubbish. It was a grotesque spectacle.

Miss Pink became aware of a small boat approaching from the settlement, the figure in the stern following Willie's progress with interest.

On the east side of the geo the cliffs were less steep and a buttress at an easy angle ran down to slanting shelves at sea level. She walked along the top of the cliffs and signalled to the boatman who, interpreting her correctly, shut down his engine and nosed into the rock.

She climbed down to the water and exchanged sharp looks with a heavy man, unshaven, with faded blue eyes, who wore the west coast garb of navy jersey and ancient beret.

'Captain Hunt?'

He nodded economically. 'And you'll be Miss Pink who's staying at the house.' His wife, a rather superior person with blue rinsed hair and upswept red glasses, waited at table.

'I wonder,' Miss Pink began, accepting his hand as she stepped into the boat and went forward to the bows, 'if you would mind running me into Scarf Geo?'

He smiled carefully. ''Tis a horrible place at the bottom, ma'am. You'll be after seeing all you want to see from the top. My, but you've put the fear o' death into that Willie. You didna even let un tip!'

They had come into the geo and he throttled back, regarding the scum round his boat benignly. 'You would be wanting to go closer, ma'am?'

'Right in, captain.'

A whiff of putrefaction drifted past. He blinked.

'Can you do it?' Miss Pink asked anxiously.

'They put dead sheeps down here!'

'Breathe through your mouth. Be quick, there's a good fellow.'

He stared at the shore as he took her in. 'What is it you've found?'

'It looks like a body.'

'Ay. Corpses do wash up in storms.'

'No doubt.'

They reached what passed for land. The boat made no healthy sound of grating on pebbles but squashed and squelched on nasty things. A basic courtesy asserted itself and he floundered after her through the muck.

'Can't stay long,' she announced stolidly. The sun beat into the back of the inlet and the flies were terrible. 'Just to satisfy ourselves. Ridiculous if it were a sheep.'

She lurched sideways against her escort.

'Watch your footing, ma'am; will ye no' go back?'

She didn't answer and she hadn't slipped; she'd nearly trodden on a green suède shoulder bag.

'God!' the captain gasped, and stopped.

Miss Pink, having been shocked by the sight of the bag, regarded the body almost with objectivity but thankful that only the legs were visible. The injuries were severe but they had not bled. Embroidered flowers showed on the rent trousers. She looked around. Willie might have tipped two or three times this morning but his shovel held comparatively little and she thought she recognised the cloth of a coat among the trash.

They returned to the boat and put out to sea. After a few hundred yards they started to take deep breaths.

'Thank you,' she said sincerely. 'You did very well.'

'How did she die, ma'am?'

'I don't know.' There was a long pause. 'How do you know who it is?'

The shock was fading and he looked sly. 'Us canna tell, but they trousers is like the lassie at Largo wore.'

'But is she missing?' Her tone was innocent, but his was equally so.

'You was looking for her this morning—with Colin. You didna find her.'

One or other of the crofters must have been watching her movements and now, like social animals, everyone knew—although they didn't know everything. Or did they? Hunt would have taken her into the geo not because she'd requested it but because he needed to know the cause of Willie's wild behaviour. She said, cautiously and untruthfully, 'By "missing" I meant disappeared; there would be nothing remarkable if she'd merely left the glen.'

'Ay. You was keen on finding her though.'

They chugged on towards the beach.

'When did you see her last?' she asked.

He reached in his pocket and, pulling out a packet of Players', offered her one. She declined, and he lit a match with his thumb nail.

'It would be after tea time,' he mused. 'Yesterday. She was sunbathing all day outside Largo. The wife said she hadna much on—' he glanced at her, '—if anything.'

'You didn't see her again?'

65

'She went indoors. It gets cold when the sun leaves that side of the glen, and there's the midges in the evening. She went in and lit the fire.'

'Did she have any visitors?'

'Not that I saw. If it's not a rude question, ma'am, why would you be so interested?'

'Good gracious! Aren't you? A dead body on your doorstep and a girl missing from the glen?'

He looked at her from under his eyebrows and decided not to push it further.

There were people on the shore. At the eastern end of the strand there were three or four groups in bright colours, campers or trippers, but working along the tide wrack towards them as the boat came in was a woman in drab clothes whom she'd met in the passages of Glen Shira House, and whom she knew as Euphemia. Miss Pink was put ashore and trudged up the sand wondering what Vera Hamlyn's cleaner was doing down here at this time of day.

'Good afternoon, Euphemia.' Behind her she heard Captain Hunt start the outboard, and looked back to see him watching them as the boat headed for Rahane.

'Good afternoon, miss.' The woman stared at her from eyes which were shrewd although filmed with age.

'You're not at the house today?' Miss Pink asked.

'I'm off now, for a while. I don't start the dinner till later. Ida Hunt does the teas.' She stopped and made pushing gestures at Captain Hunt. 'Spying on us! I do all the cooking.' This was palpably untrue; Vera Hamlyn was the cook. She stared intently at Miss Pink, waiting for her reaction.

'The food is delicious.' It was said sincerely, and Euphemia beamed. Miss Pink smiled gently.

'Which is your croft?' she asked, as if she didn't know.

The woman pointed along the shore to a single-storey cottage at the far end from Rahane. 'That's Shedog. It's a funny name, isn't it?'

'What does it mean?'

'You think it means something?' She searched Miss Pink's

face, possibly for derision. 'It's a blowy place,' she said, as if idly.

'I see. Windy. Of course, the gales will sweep straight into the loch.' Miss Pink's eyes absorbed the scenery. 'You're very exposed. But you'll see everything that goes on.'

Euphemia nodded. 'I don't miss much.' She stared at Rahane. 'You frightened that Willie MacNeill. How did you do it?'

'Not me. There's a body in the geo.'

'Is there now? How did it get there? *In* the geo?'

'Thrown down from the top.'

'Someone killed it first. No one in the glen's died natural. And anyways, they'd have to have a proper funeral. I minded my father till he died. Who is it?'

'The body's wearing trousers like the young girl wore who was camping here.'

'Where?'

Miss Pink led the way up the beach and pointed to Watkins' tent. Euphemia's eyes were blank.

'There's no girl there. It's a man.'

'She was there for a short time on Saturday.'

'*He* killed her?'

The tone was harsh, the eyes bright. Miss Pink regarded her pleasantly and Euphemia relaxed with a dazzling smile.

'She went across to Largo,' she said. 'But Colin didn't kill her.'

'How do you know?'

'I know.'

'Did you see her light go out last night?'

'Oh yes; after ten o'clock.'

'How long after?'

'I go to bed at ten—well, not quite ten; that's when I feed the Sheriff and make myself a milk drink.'

'You feed the Sheriff at ten.'

'While I'm listening to the News. I'm away about ten past. My bed faces the window. I was watching the light in Largo. It went out after I got into bed.'

'You had to drink your milk—' Her tone was calculating.

There was a flicker of anger and Miss Pink changed tactics smoothly. Her eyes lit up with amusement. 'You don't drink it in the *dark!* You'd spill it—' she paused and inspiration came, '—all over the Sheriff!'

Euphemia went off into a high cackle of laughter and this time it was Miss Pink who watched carefully. There were tears in the other's eyes.

'Scalded cat!' she cried, and Miss Pink screwed up her face in simulated amusement.

' 'Course I don't drink it in the dark.' She was sober, even thoughtful. 'You're right; I wouldna notice her light with mine —So hers went out after I blew out my candle. Probably about half past ten or a bit before.'

Miss Pink stooped, picked up a mussel shell and admired the shades of blue. 'You'll probably have a visit from the police today or tomorrow,' she said. 'Do you mind?'

Euphemia looked sly. 'It depends.' There was a gleam of excitement in her eyes. 'Here be the colonel.'

Gordon Hamlyn was striding across the dunes, his face deeply concerned.

'Is this true?' he called as he approached.

Miss Pink said that she was afraid it was.

'MacNeill's collapsed. *Is* it that young girl? He says so.'

'It looks like her trousers.'

'Good God!' He gaped at her, then looked at Euphemia sternly. 'Did you see anything?'

She was indignant. 'What would I be after seeing in the dark? I was in my bed where every self-respecting soul should be at that time of night. I told this lady what time her light went out but that didna mean anything, did it? Do you put the light out?'

He glowered at her, then turned away, taking Miss Pink's elbow. 'It's no good scolding her,' he said confidentially. 'She's not really impertinent; quite amusing at times, really.' He gave a chuckle then composed his features quickly. 'You didn't *accuse* Willie, surely?'

'No.'

'Ah. He's frightened. Said you were asking questions about

his going to Largo. I suppose there's no doubt—? He says she's in a *plastic bag!*'

'That's true. Captain Hunt took me into the geo in his boat. How quickly the bush telegraph operates in this glen! It's one of those survival bags we carry in our packs in case we're benighted.'

He stopped and stared at her. 'How was she killed?'

'I have no idea. I only saw the legs, the jeans with flowers on them. Terry Cooke had a pair like that. I didn't tell Willie about the trousers; in fact, you couldn't see them from the top.'

'That seems fishy—I mean, his saying that it's her.'

'I did tell him that she was missing.'

'Yes.' He stopped and turned. Euphemia had resumed her beach-combing and was working towards her croft.

'She knows something,' he said. 'She's a terrible liar—but not all the time. That makes it more difficult to know when she's speaking the truth. She's quite mad, of course.' He shook his head wryly. 'That's in-breeding. Accounts for a great deal, you know.'

'She never married?'

'Dear me, no.' He shot her a glance. 'That doesn't mean to say.... But Euphemia never had any children—to survive, that is. Just as well. Those lines ought to be allowed to die out, or be quietly sterilised. Perfectly simple: diagnose a suspected tumour, open 'em up, and there you are. Relatives would be relieved if they knew but—least said, soonest mended, eh? MacNeill's another: very unstable.'

'I thought that young Willie was rather a fine specimen.'

'Oh yes, indeed: fine *physical* specimen; Skye provided some of our best infantrymen in the old days. But that's the trouble: all the animal attributes and no control—not nowadays, not in civilian life. And now look what's happened.'

'What did the police say?'

He snorted and smote one hand with his fist. 'There! That's why I came to find you! They found it difficult to believe, and I had to put Willie on the line but by that time he was in tears;

they've no reserves, but then, if he ... However, as I said, they thought him drunk and asked what I made of it all, and what could I say? So I told them I'd come down and have a look myself. Was just going to take my boat out. But you've seen this body?'

'There's no doubt about it.'

He nodded. 'Would you go up and speak to the police? I told them you were a magistrate; that's right, isn't it? But Willie was the weak link, you understand. Do you think any harm's been done by the delay?'

'I doubt it.'

'How long—? When do you think he pushed her over—I mean, assuming it was a man?'

'Could a woman have carried her?'

'*Carried* her?'

'From Largo. She wouldn't have gone along those cliffs in the dark with a stranger.'

'Did it have to be in the dark?'

She stared at him. 'With Euphemia and the Hunts and all the camp site watching, not to speak of the MacNeills? How could it have been done in daylight?'

'Of course. You have a very sharp mind. Why do you say "the MacNeills" in the plural? Don't you think the lad did it?'

'No, I don't.'

And there was the light at Largo, she thought; surely the killer would never have left the light on when there was a body in the house?

Willie was hiding something. After she'd made her telephone call to the police—baldly stated it sounded merely as if a body had been washed up by the sea—Miss Pink went to the kitchen to find Vera Hamlyn and Ida Hunt sitting at a huge scrubbed table drinking tea and exchanging what by now must be weary comments. Between them Willie sprawled with his elbows on the table, a cup of tea and a glass of whisky in front of him. At her entrance, he looked truculent, but the women regarded her with expectancy, Vera rather less eagerly than Ida Hunt who was flushed with excitement.

'I've rung the police,' Miss Pink told them, and looked at the tea pot.

At that they remembered their manners and, while Ida leapt up and whisked the pot to the sink, Vera stood up and pulled out a chair.

'Please sit down. Mrs Hunt will make fresh tea. Have you had your lunch?'

'Don't worry about me—but a cup of tea will be most welcome.' She addressed them generally but her glance lingered on Willie. He glowered at her and licked his lips. He appeared to expect help from Vera and Ida but they watched him in silence, Vera with circumspection, Ida with a hint of ghoulishness.

'All right then!' he burst out. 'I *did* go across, but I didna go in! I didna go inside the door! It was closed then!'

'What time was that?' Miss Pink asked conversationally.

He shook his head, wide-eyed. 'Before eleven. The old man had gone to bed; he goes some time after ten.'

'Was there a light in Largo?'

'Not in the house, no.'

'Where, then?'

'In the burn!'

Vera and Ida looked meaningly at each other, then at Miss Pink, implying that he was drunk. He intercepted this and was furiously angry.

'I'm telling you! I stood outside the door thinking that she'd gone to bed because her light was out, and I heard a noise from the burn. I looked and saw a torch. It was a bit difficult at that moment because the Lights was very bright—' he forgot his truculence and waved an arm indicating the Northern Lights wheeling in the sky, '—so I walked towards the burn and she was washing the dishes: those aluminium sort they use camping; I heard her put them down on the rocks and I saw them shine in the torch light. I called to her and she put the light out.'

'How long did you stay?'

71

'I didna!' His voice rose again. 'She'd got a fellow with her.'

Miss Pink studied him. 'Who was it?'

'I dunno. I didna hear him speak.' His eyes sharpened suddenly.

'How did you know it was a fellow?' Miss Pink pressed.

'It musta been, mustn't it? Why would she keep quiet like that if it was a girl with her? Besides, there wasna another girl at Largo—'less someone went over from the youth hostel or the camp site, but she didna know anyone. Why would she keep quiet if it was a girl with her? It was a fellow.'

'Did you hear him speak?'

'It was just a low mumble: his voice and hers, high and low. I couldna hear the words.'

'What did you do then?'

'I turned round and went home; I wasna wanted, I could see that.'

'What do you think?'

Miss Pink and her hostess had left the kitchen and were sitting on a garden seat in front of the house. Bees hummed in a hedge of Michaelmas daisies.

'I think he was in love with her.'

'A sex crime? She wouldn't have him because of Irwin?'

'No. She was promiscuous. She wouldn't refuse Willie—he was far too attractive. Besides, she wasn't sexually attracted to Irwin.'

Vera was astonished. 'Are you sure of that?'

Miss Pink frowned. 'You don't agree?'

'I never saw them together—and I'm not sure that I'm much good at that kind of thing.' Miss Pink showed polite attention and Vera looked away, embarrassed. 'I find it better, you know, not to see what's going on—sometimes. I don't think I'd be very happy if I knew. So I'm rather naïve that way. She seemed to me very—er, obvious. You really mean the friendship with Irwin was platonic?'

'I'll amend that; there was sexual attraction, but not physical.

72

Willie would be the boy—' Miss Pink coughed. 'Quite healthy, of course.'

'What would be unhealthy?' There was a short silence. 'Watkins?'

They were very still. Out on the lawn blades of grass shivered and crumbs of rich black soil erupted above a burrowing mole.

'Watkins,' Vera repeated thoughtfully.

'Need a good cat.'

'What?'

'For the moles. Nothing like it. Euphemia's cat is called the Sheriff.'

'When did it happen?'

'After dark.'

'Euphemia wouldn't see anything then—unless she was out, of course.'

'No. She was safe in bed when it happened.'

They were quiet again for a time then Vera said: 'I wonder what his story will be?'

'He won't have one.' Miss Pink sounded casual. 'He'll have spent the evening in his tent and then: bed—or rather, sleeping bag. He *could* have an alibi.' She looked surprised at her own words.

'How could he? He didn't come up here last night. You're thinking of a girl from the camp site, or the youth hostel—who spent the night with him?'

'I imagine an alibi would have to cover all the hours of darkness.'

Lavender Maynard came walking out of the trees and across the lawn. She had a peculiar gait: flat-footed, and she moved her legs stiffly from the knee, as if her pelvic joints were frozen. She wore a large white hat and a yellow dress. She started to smile at them, then her eyes flickered from Vera's overall to Miss Pink's breeches and boots.

'Has something happened?'

'Come and sit down.' Vera patted the seat between them. '*Kenneth!*'

73

'No, no, *no!*' Vera gave a comforting little laugh. 'Nothing to bother *you.*'

Lavender seated herself and her colour came back. 'Stupid of me, but when they climb—but of course, Colonel Hamlyn climbs.... It's different when you do it yourself; and then, taking a woman guide! I wouldn't worry if he would employ men but a woman's no good in emergencies, is she?' She shrugged. 'I mean: they go to pieces.'

The others looked bland.

'But something's wrong,' she went on more naturally.

Vera glanced at Miss Pink who said, 'Terry Cooke has had an accident.'

Lavender licked her lips. 'What kind of accident?'

'She's dead.'

'Oh yes? Well, that's bad.' Only her mouth moved. 'What happened?'

'The body was put in a plastic bag and dropped down Scarf Geo.'

'That—is—unbelievably—horrible.' The voice was expressionless. 'Why are you telling me this?'

'You asked.'

'You're being deliberately callous. What significance does it have for me?'

'None,' Vera said chidingly. 'Miss Pink isn't callous, just practical; she's getting it over as quickly as possible.'

'I see.' Lavender addressed herself to Miss Pink. 'You do know that Kenneth and I share a room?'

Vera looked stupid. Miss Pink stared, then nodded in comprehension: 'And you don't take sleeping pills?'

'I do, as a matter of fact. When was she killed?'

Vera gave an exasperated sigh and went indoors.

'What's wrong with her?' Lavender asked histrionically.

'She's tired. We've had a busy hour or so.'

'I didn't come down for lunch. I was resting. What happened? Was she killed at Largo?'

Miss Pink recounted the facts. She didn't say that when she left Irwin that morning she had started to wonder where Terry

Cooke might be if she had never left the glen, nor that she was not concerned with pollution when she first looked down Scarf Geo. At the end of the account Lavender observed that the girl had brought it on herself. Miss Pink stood up.

'Where are you going?' the other asked suspiciously.

Miss Pink went in the porch and emerged with her rucksack. She didn't answer but waved a hand and strode up the drive.

Chapter 7

FROM A VANTAGE point Miss Pink raked the slopes above Glen Shira through binoculars and, having located her quarry, met the Lindsays and Watkins above the waterfall. She made no pretence that the encounter was an accident but there seemed little to be gleaned from their initial reactions to her appearance.

Betty seemed pleased to see her, Watkins amused; Lindsay's expression was, as usual, faintly anxious, but it was impossible to decide whether this originated in his difficulty with human relationships or merely from the fear of putting his foot in a rabbit hole.

After an exchange of cursory greetings (as if they really had met by accident), she accompanied them to the lip of the ravine, where they halted and looked back at the waterfall dropping daintily down the rock. Betty remarked that they needed rain.

A small sigh escaped Miss Pink and the younger woman turned, her expression questioning, then alert. She glanced from Miss Pink to the glen. The road and Glen Shira House were hidden by a convex slope but they could see across the mouth of the valley to Largo and Rahane and, following the green shelf westwards, it was possible to make out Scarf Geo.

'Terry Cooke has gone,' Miss Pink said.

Watkins looked startled, then relieved. 'That's a pleasant welcome at the end of the day.'

Lindsay shot him a glance. Betty asked, 'Gone where?'

The guide gave a snort of laughter. 'What the hell does that matter so long as she's off my back?' A thought struck him. 'You do mean she's left the glen?' he asked of Miss Pink.

'No. She's dead.'

Betty gasped. There was a pause, then she said coldly, 'You mean—drowned? A swimming accident? Or did someone take her climbing...? Or—' She looked down at the ravine.

'Her body is in Scarf Geo.'

'Oh—h!' The exclamation—of enlightenment, and drawn out —came from Lindsay, and Miss Pink turned to him. His face was clear and boyish and he smiled at her weakly. His forehead was damp. 'Suicide,' he observed.

'That is possible. But if so, then she died in some other place, because the body is in a survival bag.'

'I don't understand,' Betty said.

'One of those large plastic bags that we carry— You probably have one in your pack now.' She addressed the guide.

'Yes,' he said quickly, 'I have.'

Betty said with deliberation, 'You mean someone put her in a bag? But that would mean murder.'

'Not necessarily.' Miss Pink was brisk. 'She could have met with an accident or committed suicide and then someone put the body in a bag and dropped it down Scarf Geo. There are reasons for people covering up a death, or otherwise confusing the issue. Bodies are often moved after car accidents for example, and, in the case of an illegal abortion, it's important to get the body off the premises as quickly as possible.'

'But that doesn't hold in this case,' Lindsay pointed out. 'She wasn't pregnant.'

'How do you know?' Miss Pink asked with interest. He was dumbfounded. Watkins swallowed painfully.

Betty said reasonably, 'In those tight pants it would have shown; she was as flat as a board.'

'I never saw her in pants,' Miss Pink said, and watched Betty's face freeze. 'In the dress which she was wearing on Saturday evening it would be difficult to tell.'

Watkins started to grin. Betty looked from him to her husband and said meaningly, 'I think we'd better get down.'

She touched Lindsay's arm and gestured towards the glen. The guide watched them go, then turned and joined Miss Pink in contemplation of the waterfall. When she sat down on a bank he followed suit, then asked, 'When was she killed?'

'I don't know.'

He moved impatiently. 'When was she found then?'

'About midday today.'

'And who saw her last? Alive?'

She looked at him and he added quickly, 'I mean, who apart from the killer?'

'It seems that a man was talking to her some time before eleven last night—'

'Who told you that?'

'Why do you ask?'

'Well, naturally I'm interested. He could be lying, could be trying to protect himself.... It's likely that the fellow who told you she had a visitor last night, could be the killer, yes?'

'I didn't say my informant was a man.'

'So it was a woman.' He turned his head. The Lindsays were out of sight. 'Could be.' He looked at her with an expression of candour. 'I always thought she liked young girls. That's the trouble between her and her husband; you've noticed it, of course. She's wearing the trousers in that set-up, no mistake about it, but I never thought it went any further: outside the family, like. But there's no reason why those sort shouldn't be the same as everyone else—I mean, they've got their appetites, haven't they? And she didn't—doesn't—give a damn about her husband; there's nothing between them at all. You could tell she was attracted to Terry on Saturday night; she was so spiteful. Love-hate relationship, that's what it was.'

'How curious that you should put that interpretation on it.' Miss Pink was thoughtful. 'Granted she's a powerful woman, but I thought her very feminine at heart.' She laughed deprecatingly. 'In fact, I would have said that she was very much attracted to yourself.'

His mouth stretched in a nervous grin. 'Yeah, she was a nuisance, like that.' There was a brief pause. 'I couldn't shake her off; middle-aged women are far worse than kids. They get infatuated; a lot of it's the glamour of the job. She used to come down to the camp site in the evenings.' He stopped as if waiting for questions.

'Alone?'

'Difficult to remember.' He grinned again. 'I had a lot of visitors. She made a number of suggestions to me—propositions, you'd call them rightly.'

'What was her husband's reaction?'

'Oh, he didn't care; he'd be used to it.'

'You didn't think this was an isolated instance, then?'

'Come again?'

'She was often infatuated with younger men?'

He drew a breath. 'There were several things—contributory factors.' He smiled, pleased with the term. 'There was the heat, she often remarked on it: made us fed-up—I mean, we wanted to concentrate on the *climbing*. It would be her age, I guess; that would be another factor. And then they'd never had any children. She wanted to mother me—and him, but that's unhealthy, isn't it?' He grimaced in distaste. 'I don't know why I'm telling you all this. I've always found her a bit of a drag. I've been guiding them for years now; they're quite good climbers but I must admit she's getting embarrassing lately; not enough to make me refuse to guide them any more but little things—some of them more than little: make your hair stand on end, the things she says. Everything had a double meaning, you know? And a party's pretty intimate on the hill; you've got to strike a delicate balance if a situation's not to get out of hand. I don't mind admitting that with Mrs Lindsay I'd got to the stage where I wondered if she was round the twist. I'd not wanted to take them this year and I'm definitely going to find a way to get out of taking them next year.' He lifted his hand and stared blankly at a piece of lousewort clutched between his fingers. 'None of this surprises me,' he added.

'Ah, good evening!' Ken Maynard came into the cocktail lounge, still bouncing with energy after his day on the hill. 'Just in time for a quick one, Gordon; two lagers, please.'

'Make it pints,' Madge amended, following him. 'It's humid

today; I feel dehydrated. Good evening, Miss Pink; I didn't see you in the corner.'

'Have you had a good day?'

'An easy day for her,' Maynard responded. 'We didn't put the rope on until we were coming off the third pinnacle. What did you do?'

It was the ritual question. They were only interested in their beer at this moment.

'I found Terry Cooke's body.'

Maynard looked moderately startled. 'Found Terry's *what?*' Madge regarded her warily.

'Body,' Miss Pink repeated. 'She's dead.'

Maynard stared at her, then turned to Hamlyn. 'Is that true?' The hotelier nodded mutely.

'How did she die?' Madge asked.

'We don't know.' Miss Pink reflected that by now it was likely that a number of people knew, not to mention the one person who had known all along.

'She was murdered,' Maynard said coldly.

'How do you know that?' She felt a *frisson* of excitement as one person came out in the open.

'Because only that could explain your peculiar—and discourteous—method of breaking the news. It's ghastly, but you made no effort to cushion the shock, because you want our reactions. And that presupposes not merely—God, "merely"!—murder, but that there is some doubt or—' he regarded her keenly, '—or a lot of doubt, as to who killed her.'

Madge was frowning. She looked tired. 'Do you have any more details?' she asked.

Miss Pink told them how the body had been found.

'Why a survival bag?'

Hamlyn and Miss Pink were silent.

Maynard said flatly, 'Because he had to carry her from Largo. If the body wasn't wrapped it would leave traces on his clothing, or on the pack frame that he must have used to carry her. Also it's possible that he thought that plastic doesn't take fingerprints.' He grinned at Miss Pink unpleasantly.

80

'Does it?' Madge asked her.

'Yes, but he could have worn gloves.'

'It means a climber,' the guide postulated. 'A survival bag and a pack frame. Was there a frame near the body?'

'I didn't see one, but then it could have been covered by rubbish. The reason the body wasn't, was that it slid off the plastic, presumably.'

'Why are you so certain about the frame?' Hamlyn asked.

Madge regarded him with good-natured contempt. 'A fireman's lift? All that way?' She turned to the others. 'But only a climber would think of a pack frame. There wouldn't be any traces.... But he's lost his survival bag. It's simple, isn't it? Whoever can't produce a bag—'

'It's not so simple as that,' Miss Pink demurred. 'A person who has no bag today could say he never had one.'

'Unless someone knew he had one,' Maynard pointed out. 'But then he would have come prepared with two bags.'

'"Would have come",' Miss Pink repeated, 'to the island? You think it was premeditated?' There was a dead silence. Her eyes became abstracted, then sharpened. 'And working on the lines of personal equipment is no help at all,' she went on, 'there's all the gear in the Rescue Post.' Mountain Rescue equipment was stored in a stable at the back of the house.

'You'd better see if anything's missing,' Maynard told Hamlyn. 'What's your security like?'

The other glowered, but seeing Miss Pink's eyes on him, muttered unhappily, 'The stable's kept locked, but the key hangs in the passage inside the back door—with a tag marked Mountain Rescue Post. We don't lock the back door until we go to bed.'

'So it could have been anyone,' Madge said.

'Hardly anyone,' Maynard corrected. 'Survival bags are kept folded. Only a climber would know that they were big enough to get a body inside; only a climber would know that they were bags. It's assuming too much to imagine a non-climbing tripper "borrowing" the key and taking just a plastic bag out of all the valuable gear lying around in that stable—against the time when he's going to need it.' He looked at Hamlyn. 'You'd better go and take an inventory.'

'It wouldn't prove anything. The pack frame will have been put back, and I'm not particular about listing the numbers of small items like plastic bags.'

'You'd make a good quarter-master,' Maynard said acidly.

Detective Chief Inspector Merrick was tall and thin with hair which, having receded in a wide central swathe, made his face appear longer than it was. An impression of astuteness wasn't contradicted by his other features; he was all angles: chin, nose and pointed ears, and he shone with a kind of bony cleanliness.

His sergeant—a man called Ivory—was equally tall, but broad. Miss Pink always had the feeling that policemen's wives knew little about diet; the only thin ones were those who would be thin in any circumstances—like Merrick. Another thought came to her as Merrick introduced Ivory; weight and fat were usually correlated with geniality but it was seldom that one met genial detectives. Despite his double chin, Ivory had sharp eyes and a narrow mouth. He hailed from Glasgow and looked like a successful ironmaster. She thought he would be good with professional criminals. Merrick looked as if he'd be good anywhere.

It was now nine o'clock. It had been a strange evening for the residents of Glen Shira House. By way of the bush telegraph they'd been made aware of the movements of the police, but not of the details, and they'd tried to fill the gaps in their knowledge by speculation. During the afternoon the boats belonging to the settlement, directed by Captain Hunt, had taken policemen to Scarf Geo, and there were strange people along the top of the cliffs. There was a uniformed man on duty outside Largo and men in plain clothes coming and going. There was a rumour that fingerprints were being taken. After dinner the police asked to see Miss Pink.

They were in the writing room. From the beginning it was clear that she was the one person who could be eliminated as a suspect, and that Merrick was going to take full advantage of her position and her knowledge. She'd been three days in the glen, had made contact with everyone except old MacNeill, and now she told them what she'd learned. It was a strange recital for, with hindsight, almost everything that had happened possessed significance and it was difficult for her not to be side-tracked by her own revelations.

Ivory took notes but not many; she realised that since these were scanty there was indeed a good brain under Merrick's high skull. Her formal statement—relating to the finding of the body—was all that was taken down carefully, but it seemed sparse. It was astonishing how concise one could be about death. Merrick asked more questions about the living people. She had a sudden impression, perhaps erroneous, that despite the wild setting they thought this was a stereotyped crime.

Merrick, sitting at the writing table, regarded the notebook in front of him and read aloud: 'Watkins, Irwin, Hamlyn, Lindsay, Maynard.' He looked up. 'Are we right in assuming that a woman couldn't have carried the body? Climbers must be very strong. Is it not possible? What did she weigh? Eight and a half, nine stone?'

'Nearer nine,' Miss Pink ventured. 'That's—one hundred and twenty six pounds. A woman accustomed to carrying heavy loads could do it, but it's over a mile from Largo to Scarf Geo, and we'd all know if there were a woman as strong as that around ... surely?' There was a pause during which the build of the women in the glen passed before her mind's eye. She continued without expression, 'Also I'm sure she'd need assistance to get the body on the frame, and to hoist the frame on her back....'

By now it was generally accepted that, in view of the plastic bag which would make the load incredibly slippery—as Madge had suggested—a pack frame must have been used as well. Ivory had checked the rescue equipment with Hamlyn but no frames were missing. That was not conclusive; it could have been taken and returned. Hamlyn couldn't be sure about the survival bags.

'So,' Merrick continued, reverting to his list, 'the body was probably too heavy for a woman to carry. That leaves us with these men.'

'Only those five?'

He looked at her keenly. 'These to interview, ma'am. There are three more: Hunt and the MacNeills. We've had preliminary talks with them.'

'They're the crofters.'

'The more important people had to wait until I arrived.' It was said dryly. So it was the preliminaries which lesser ranks had been engaged on during the afternoon and early evening. It was dark now and high tide. The body was protected by a plastic tent and was being watched over by two men on top of the cliffs. Since the geo could only be approached by sea, and oars and outboards had been removed from the boats, there was no need to place a guard right on that awful tip. In any event, said Merrick, it was most unlikely that the killer would approach the body at this stage, when it had been photographed and the plastic bag treated for prints, but one had to observe the letter of the law.

The body had been examined by a doctor. There were bruises on the throat which suggested strangulation, and it was almost certain that the other injuries had been caused after death, from the effects of the fall. Nothing was certain of course; they would have to wait for the pathologist's report. However, there were indications. The body was fully clothed: in a pink halter top under a black jumper, and the jeans were fastened. It was not, on the face of it, a picture of rape. A search in the rubbish had revealed the bedding roll and a coat in addition to the shoulder bag. Even the flip-flops, the lilac dress and the contents of the plastic carriers (and the carriers) were found. Irwin had been ferried out to find and identify these effects. They had found no pack frame in the geo.

'You've told us about these five men,' Merrick was saying, 'as they appear to you. We'll go over them briefly to see if I've read you correctly, and then I think we'll call it a night. Let's start with Watkins. Stop me if you disagree. He's forty-ish, powerful, running to fat; lazy, bad-mannered, and a bad guide. What is it, ma'am?'

'Perhaps not bad technically, not a bad climber, just clumsy; it's his relations with his clients that are unethical.'

'Can you elaborate?'

She thought for a moment. 'It's difficult to find an analogy. The point is that the activity is potentially dangerous—and emotional relationships destroy objectivity. So in this context such relationships are irresponsible. In putting his clients at risk he is a bad guide.'

'You see why we need you. To continue: Watkins drinks heavily, he used violence on Terry Cooke and appears to have emptied her purse—of less than a pound, and he's earning something like ten pounds a day excluding expenses.' Merrick and Ivory exchanged looks. 'We see a lot of violence and a lot more petty thieving. I don't like a man who knocks women about and then steals a few coppers from her. It's not fitting in this environment.' Miss Pink's mouth twitched. He went on, 'The relationship between him and each of his current clients is also odd. Dear me, what a peculiar triangle for the Cuillin. What else was there?'

Ivory pretended to look at his notes. 'An inveterate liar.'

'Was that my word—inveterate?' Miss Pink was ingenuous. 'That conversation I had with him this afternoon was bizarre; he appeared to assume that the killer was a man, then followed me rather too closely when I pointed out I had not mentioned the killer's sex, and so jumped to the conclusion it was a woman. Was that stupidity or—'

She stopped. Merrick said, 'Or a clever man pretending to be stupid. I don't know; I wasn't there.'

'Low cunning,' Miss Pink said thoughtfully. 'Then there was his suggestion that Betty Lindsay was a Lesbian and so she could be the killer, but when I said that I'd thought that Betty was attracted to him, either vanity or prudence got the better of him, and he went off on that tack, but maintaining that the attachment was neurotic on Betty's part. I got a strong impression that he was building fantasies as he went along. He would start with a lie or an innuendo and then get carried away. Definitely not a clever man, I would say.'

'Unless diabolically clever, ma'am.'

'Not George Watkins. Just self-centred, I imagine. If he has any feeling for anyone, it's for himself. I can't see him taking the *trouble* to go across to Largo.'

'Perhaps she went to him,' Ivory said, and the others looked at him, Miss Pink thinking that he could be right; so many victims had a compulsive need for their predator.

Merrick was following his own line of thought. 'Hardly rape,' he mused, 'unless he dressed her afterwards. Unusual though. But then it's unusual to remove the body; you'd expect him to leave it lying, but perhaps he thought it would be covered by rubbish and not found, at least till he'd got away. But no one has left the glen since last evening, excluding Maynard, who did, but came back. What puzzles you, ma'am?'

'I'm wondering why you've not mentioned young MacNeill.'

'Haven't we? You think he's a strong suspect?'

'I thought you would think so.'

'You think we always follow the obvious lines. True enough. We've spent quite a while with young Willie. I haven't seen him myself, mind, but I've read his statement and talked to the officers who saw him. There doesn't seem to be any discrepancy with what he told you in the kitchen. Not a very articulate lad, particularly by the time our people reached him, but shock could account for some of his behaviour. We have his reactions on finding the body from you. He could have been acting, like Watkins. Low cunning is sometimes sufficient to carry through an act. If they have the nerve to stick to a story, it can be very difficult to break them down. There's that tale about him going to Largo and hearing the girl washing dishes in the company of a man. If it's true, who's the fellow? If it's not true, why tell us?' He looked at his sergeant.

'Because someone saw him over there,' Ivory said patiently.

'Then why doesn't he identify the fellow? He's a suspect too.'

'He only heard the man mumbling,' Miss Pink said. 'I agree

with you, Mr Merrick; the story must be true because there's no reason why he should make it up. If anything, it incriminates him. After all, his father almost certainly knew the lad was out, but his story will agree with the son's.'

'He doesn't say he heard Willie come in. He says he was fast asleep and heard nothing.'

'Confidence,' she hazarded. 'He knows his son didn't do it and doesn't need alibis.'

'But that business of dumping the rubbish on top of the body,' Merrick continued. 'It's suspicious—although all the locals, and the people staying here, knew he'd be tipping sooner or later. If he wasn't the killer, he was certainly being used as an unwitting accessory.'

'It could have had significance,' she murmured.

'How's that, ma'am?'

'Hatred. Like multiple stab wounds after death. To put the body on a tip might have been choice, not expediency.'

He thought about that for a while then leaned forward with his elbows on the table. Miss Pink was in an easy chair on the other side. 'If it wasn't rape, did sex have any bearing on the murder?' he asked.

'I think so. You never saw her.'

'What did she look like?'

'She was the kind of girl people turn round and look at in the street, even if she's wearing the dullest clothes. She would excite passion in any man, and many women. Either love or hate but never indifference.'

'Indeed?'

'It wasn't only her appearance but the things she said. She seemed unaware of the *nature* of the reactions she roused in people; she was rather stupid, you know: a very dangerous combination. One sees so many pretty girls in the courts who are not really delinquents, just innocent animals. Unfortunately they're usually found by weak or wicked people and get into trouble before they have time to find the kind of people who might see to it that they come to no harm. But of course, they can't tell the difference.'

87

Merrick's eyes were grim but he didn't follow that line. 'Who's next?' he asked, looking at his list. 'Irwin. In his twenties, a good guide but doesn't possess formal qualifications, which puts him on the wrong side of our host, who is old-fashioned. You say Irwin was fond of the girl, took her in when Watkins threw her out....' He nodded to himself. 'We don't know much about Irwin really, do we? Except that on the night of the murder he was allegedly sleeping in a tent on his own not many miles away.'

'But he'd have no reason to—'

There was a knock at the door and Gordon Hamlyn entered with a tea tray. 'I guessed you'd be needing this,' he said with a self-congratulatory air. He placed the tray on the table, nodded at Merrick and, without invitation, started to set out the cups.

'I understand you climb, sir?' Merrick said, and Miss Pink remembered that Hamlyn was on his list.

'I can still lead a Severe competently. Do you climb?'

'No.' The inspector looked at Miss Pink.

'A Severe is quite hard,' she explained. 'The colonel is a well-known mountaineer.'

'So you'll know all about equipment,' Merrick mused as the other started to pour out the tea. He gave Miss Pink a small smile. 'I'd appreciate a second opinion on some of these points, sir. Now, this business of the disposal: we don't often come across cases where bodies are carried so far—manually, but climbers must be used to the weight of a body?'

'There's a confusion here between climbers and rescuers.' Hamlyn had handed round tea and biscuits, and now he settled himself in a chair. 'Climbers are familiar with the weight of other climbers when there's a slip or a fall, but you have to remember that the fallen man is then alive and conscious and capable of helping himself. Of course, I'm speaking of the normal run of events, you understand, not a serious or fatal fall. All climbers are familiar with the weight of a second on the rope—but that is not in the same category as the full weight of a body. That is, if you'll forgive the pun, a dead weight.' He leaned back and regarded Merrick with satisfaction.

'Carried many?' the latter asked with an air of childish curiosity.

The other nodded. 'A great many, but never for long distances on my own. We usually manage to find at least six men for the stretcher. But I have, on occasions, had to hoist a body about unaided: in difficult places and before the full team arrives at the site of the accident. They are very heavy indeed, you may take my word for that—and damnably awkward: floppy before *rigor*, stiff as a board afterwards.'

'I can believe it. What an interesting life you lead. Do a power of good too. Bodies are the business of the police by rights. Without Mountain Rescue teams, there'd have to be a special department trained to deal with violent death in the mountains. The taxpayer's saved thousands of pounds by voluntary rescue teams.'

Hamlyn's face was stiff with embarrassment. He gave a loud, barking cough. 'We do what we can. How can I help you here?'

'George Watkins,' Merrick said dreamily. 'Is he a professional guide?'

'Yes.'

'Do his job well?'

'I'd rather not answer that one.'

The inspector didn't comment on that. 'Colin Irwin?' he went on.

'You want my professional opinion? He's not a qualified guide. One of the long-haired brigade: a squatter in MacNeill's cottage across the river—well, of course you know Largo! What am I thinking of? MacNeill would have allowed him to stay there to spite me, I dare say. They know how I feel about hooligans and hippies.'

'Been making himself a nuisance to you, has he—Irwin? An alcoholic?'

'I won't have him in my bar.'

'Ah. Drugs then, is it?'

'They're all on drugs.'

'Tell me what he's done to annoy you, colonel.'

Hamlyn re-crossed his legs. 'Nothing specific—no need for

that. But you must understand that climbing is an extremely dangerous game, and guides must be highly qualified. They're subjected to the most stringent tests and examinations by the Mountaineering Council before they're granted their certificates and allowed to practise. We have two guides in the glen at this moment and whatever they are otherwise—one of them, that is —there's no getting away from it: they *are* qualified guides. Irwin is nothing but a long-haired layabout: an ordinary climber out to make an easy buck. I heard that he's actually been refused his certificates, and I wouldn't mind betting that this was because of his manner. Clients are particular about the fellows they employ on the hill. They like to see discipline, and that's something that Irwin is a stranger to: discipline.'

'You have deduced that from conversation with him?'

'I haven't conversed with the man. You've only got to look at him.' He grimaced with disgust. 'He wears his hair in a kind of band.' He looked at the others meaningly. 'My wife calls it an Alice band.' His face was suddenly expressionless. 'I've seen him tie it back in a ribbon.'

'And the dead girl: would you say she was a female counter-part of Irwin?'

He gave the matter thought, then shook his head decisively. 'No, not at all. She was neat and clean.' He smiled wryly. 'Out-landishly dressed, of course, but very charming, and so pleasantly old-fashioned. Wore a long skirt. These short skirts have led to a lot of crime in my opinion. I could be biased but it's all part of the permissive attitudes nowadays. Fashion isn't the least of it; there's the media with public performances on television of the most private acts, and this, sir, is all exploitation of the masses by a few. . . .' He came forward in his chair. 'The collapse of every civilisation has been preceded by decadence, were you aware of that?' He leaned back and surveyed Merrick and Ivory. 'That's why the police are powerless, why the crime rate is rising and you can do nothing to contain it—because decadence is starting at the top. This country is no democracy, sir; it's run by men who are so anxious for power that they'll do anything to please the voters. Britain is ruled by the masses, with a few hundred puppets at the top, and all decadent, every one of them.'

'Exactly,' Merrick said, his eyes glazed. 'And what's your remedy?'

Suddenly Hamlyn slumped and sighed deeply. 'I sympathise with you, indeed I do; it's uphill work all the way, and no corporal punishment, no death penalty.' He smiled at Miss Pink with charm. 'And if I say the magistrates are too lenient, I shall lose this good lady's favour.'

'So you're suggesting that the murder had some association with decadence?' Merrick suggested.

'It sounds silly, put that way, but it was preceded by the most outrageous behaviour which, I admit now, should have been reported to you at the time.'

'Yes? Who was at fault there?'

Hamlyn appeared confused. 'Perhaps all of us. I believe we were all aware that the girl had been badly treated, yet we did nothing about it.'

'You're referring to last Saturday night?'

'Of course.' He looked at the inspector as if the man were mad. 'Nothing like that has occurred in this glen before, not in our time at all events. A man who can hit a woman is capable of anything, sir! And to continue beating her after the first blow, after he's seen the damage he's already inflicted, that is sheer sadism!'

'He beat her for some considerable time, did he?' Merrick flicked back through his notebook as if looking for a reference. 'We don't seem to have a description of the injuries,' he mused. Hamlyn waited attentively. 'What *were* her injuries?' Merrick asked, still leafing through the pages, then he looked up.

Hamlyn said, 'You were addressing me? I didn't see her after the Saturday evening.'

Merrick looked flustered. 'I must get people's movements straight. I think we'd better do some work on that now.' He glanced at Ivory and smiled at Hamlyn who, recognising that this was dismissal, got up reluctantly and went out.

Miss Pink and the inspector regarded each other.

'How stupid is he?' Merrick asked.

She was thoughtful. 'Stupidity is seldom consistent, is it? People will have blind spots in one direction, particularly where human relationships are concerned, and yet be perceptive and intelligent in other directions. Look at wives and husbands: devoted wives who are completely blind to husbands who are rogues, oafs, misers—you know the kind of thing—and yet quite good judges of character or at least, high-principled, where other people are concerned. It's a kind of dual morality.'

'Those are women blinded by passion and, as you say, not uncommon. I was talking about Hamlyn, ma'am.'

'I'm sorry; I was side-tracked.... Hamlyn? Oh yes; stupid in one direction, you see: in his view of society, but then surely, it's only a matter of degree? He's way out on the right wing. A lot of old regular officers are that way inclined.'

'Heaven preserve me from them.' He sighed and looked at his watch. 'We have to be up early. Let's have a look at the last two on the list. Andrew Lindsay; now he's the man who's employing the execrable Watkins—and the only time Lindsay is happy is in Watkins' company. Otherwise he's morose, nervous, preoccupied. His wife is a dominating lady who is treated abominably by Watkins when they're climbing. She's a superior climber to her husband—does he resent that, I wonder? You suspect a relationship between the two men. How does the wife react to that?'

'She appears unconcerned. It could be as Watkins suggested: that she'd like to mother both of them.'

Even Ivory was startled at that. Merrick recovered himself and wondered what this triangle might have to do with the deceased. No one helped him. 'And then there's Kenneth Maynard,' he went on. ' "Porn?" ' he read from his notebook. He addressed Ivory, 'Why pornography?'

The sergeant coughed meaningly and one nostril twitched. 'Woman's magazine,' he prompted.

Merrick glanced at Miss Pink who mistook the nature of the cue. 'I have no more facts than I gave you.' She was apologetic.

'Fifty-ish,' Merrick said, out of his head, not from his notebook. 'An enthusiastic climber, employs expert lady guide, not a *femme fatale*—' his audience was expressionless, '—his somewhat older wife is in ill-health and doesn't climb. Frets, perhaps?' He looked at the table. 'A liking for young girls?'

'Not Lavender,' Miss Pink murmured.

He looked at her reproachfully. 'Maynard.'

'Not apparent.'

'Powerful?'

'Only moderately.'

'He climbs, so he carries heavy loads but not, as the colonel explained at length, dead weights. And he brought the girl to the glen.'

'That meeting must have been coincidence. Moreover, there'd be no opportunity for dalliance in Lavender's presence. And I'm sure he didn't meet her again.'

'Ma'am!' He was pained and she looked guilty.

'I'm sorry; I must be getting tired.' She amended the statement. 'He spoke to her in the cocktail lounge on Saturday evening but to my knowledge he didn't meet her again.'

'That's better.' He nodded as if a promising pupil had redeemed a mistake. 'What time did Maynard go to bed that night—I mean, Monday night of course? You went up at eight-thirty.' He looked at Ivory. 'So—we want the movements of these five men from six on Monday evening until six on Tuesday morning.' He saw the question in Miss Pink's eyes. 'The last independent witness to have seen her alive is yourself, ma'am: about six, you said, when she went inside Largo with young MacNeill. And it gets light about six in the morning. After that the killer had to be in his bed or somewhere else equally innocent. Sunrise is at seven. The body was put down Scarf Geo in the dark.'

She nodded and looked diffident. 'Were you implying that Maynard's magazine was pornographic?'

'No, ma'am.' He tapped his notebook. 'I had put a query against the term.' Ivory was frowning fiercely. 'But Mr Ivory wouldn't query it.'

'Permissive,' the sergeant observed. 'Only just keeps clear of the Obscene Publications Act.'

'Really?' Miss Pink was surprised.

'Article on—er—'

'Eunuchs,' Merrick supplied equably.

'With pictures.' Ivory glowered. 'Made a lot of trouble in the Highlands.'

'I would have thought, with lambs, and bullocks—'

'They're different,' Ivory said.

She was silent for a moment while Merrick started to gather up his papers, then she said abstractedly: 'Yes, it is a publication that does sail close to the wind and now I think I see a correlation—between his work and his climbing. I'd have thought that exploiting sex was the antithesis of climbing. But he's an intelligent man, not your typical flesh-peddler—' their eyes widened at her, '—he needs the hills. Poor fellow,' she mused, 'it must be very hard on him.'

'Hard enough to kill, ma'am?'

She looked at them as if she were surfacing from an anaesthetic. 'To kill? Kill Terry Cooke? Why should he?'

'Oh, come now!' Merrick was impatient. They were all tired. 'Here's a man all mixed up with sex: makes his living out of it, married to a woman who's probably mad with jealousy because he spends all day—and sometimes whole holidays—alone with an attractive girl thirty years younger than herself.... Are you going to tell me he hasn't had an affair with Madge Fraser?'

'No—but I do feel that the murderer was a passionate person and I don't think Maynard has much feeling for women, not in that way.'

'Lust,' Ivory put in. 'She was sunbathing nude.' He glanced at the window but the curtains were drawn against the night. 'All right in France perhaps but it's not right here, is it? You saw her; anyone else could have seen her from the upper floor of this house—or anywhere else, come to that; could have seen it as an invitation. He went across after dark, she didn't want him, she screamed.'

'No one heard a scream.'

94

'She tried to scream, ma'am.'

She escaped from the writing room at last, but she was to have one more encounter before the night was over. As she started upstairs a door slammed loudly on the bedroom floor, and then another. She shook her head in disapproval, reflecting that good manners were going to the dogs even in Glen Shira House. She stopped at a book case outside her room and studied the spines of paperbacks.

Suddenly the lavatory next door was flushed and Madge emerged looking shocked and angry. She was a peculiar colour as if she were pale under her tan. Although she saw Miss Pink, her expression didn't change. She blundered along the corridor to her room and slammed that door. Forgetting all about books, Miss Pink entered her room, then paused and turned the key.

Chapter 8

OVERNIGHT THE WEATHER changed. In the morning there were still no clouds but the light was harder and the air less fresh. Miss Pink went down for breakfast to find the place seething with hysteria. At the foot of the stairs Vera Hamlyn and Madge Fraser confronted each other, engaged in an altercation so intense that they seemed oblivious of the guests.

'... in the circumstances I have no option,' Madge was saying. 'But I'm not leaving the glen; I'm going to camp by the waterfall until I've done the ridge.'

'Excuse me.' Miss Pink was trying to squeeze past the guide who moved but didn't look at her. Miss Pink went through the door of the cocktail lounge to encounter the fervid eyes of Lavender Maynard who was standing, incongruously at this hour, at the cleared bar. From the hall Vera's voice was brittle: 'I would have thought the least you could do was to leave the island.'

Madge said, with equal coldness, 'For one thing I doubt if the police would let me go, for another, you don't really think I'm going to come down here and bother you in the evenings, do you? I'll only be there a couple of days.'

'For God's sake!' Vera exclaimed. 'Don't you realise what you're doing? Please go.'

The tone was desperate but there was no response. Someone walked away, to be followed, after a pause, by the other. Lavender stared with ghoulish triumph at Miss Pink who turned and went out. There was no one in the hall.

At the far end of the dining room Maynard was talking

96

urgently to Madge who stared out of the window with a stony face. Miss Pink sat at her table and heard heels on the parquet behind her. Lavender stalked past and sat down, her back like a ramrod. Maynard joined her and at that moment Ida Hunt came hurrying in with their coffee, saying good morning cheerfully all round.

The Lindsays entered, wearing climbing clothes, and now all except Madge speculated in low voices on the extent to which their movements were going to be restricted. They appealed to Miss Pink who could tell them nothing on that score.

Breakfast threatened to be disrupted by the arrival of several cars obviously containing reporters but Hamlyn—very much the colonel at this moment—came quickly through the hall to shepherd them back to the gravel sweep. Voices were raised and there were references to private property and Fascism, but the cars went away again.

After breakfast Sergeant Ivory asked Miss Pink if she could spare a moment for the inspector. She found Merrick sitting in the writing room as if he'd been there all night. He stood up at her entrance.

'Good morning, ma'am; I trust you had an undisturbed night? Would you be available in about two hours' time? You weren't proposing to go climbing?' He was most courteous. She agreed to stay in the glen that morning.

'Yes.' He breathed a sigh of relief as if he had been dreading obstruction. 'I'm going to see these five this morning: the men on the list, and get their movements.... The pathologist's report isn't going to help with the time of death because we don't know when she last ate. Willie can't help us; she didn't mention supper when he was there early on. I understand you're friendly with Euphemia Morrison, ma'am?'

'With Euphemia!'

He smiled. 'Yes, she appears to be a stranger to the truth. That's the problem. But she did tell us you were "a proper lady", which implies respect. We can't get anything out of her except obvious lies otherwise. Do you think you might do better? Her cottage faces Largo. She might have seen something *after* the light went out: might have seen it lit again perhaps, or a torch moving along the top of the cliffs—or anywhere else.' He looked doubtful. 'You might have some trouble. She threatened our people; claimed acquaintance with the sheriff.'

'Well, I don't think she meant that.'

'She appears to be far from normal.'

'Where do you suggest I talk to her?'

'You'll find her in her cottage. She's handed in her notice for some reason. You'll have all the privacy you need down there.'

Shedog was an old black house with stone walls and a roof of rushes, the thatch being protected from the wicked winds by ropes weighted with large stones. There was a squat chimney at either end and two sash windows with white trim. The door, also painted white, was ajar and propped open by a chunk of quartzite.

Miss Pink's knock sounded uncanny in the stillness. There was a stirring in the depths and Euphemia came through the wood-lined passage, her expression carefully composed to welcome her caller. Ostensibly Miss Pink was concerned that the other was not at the big house but Euphemia explained with dignity that her affairs were private and if the poliss wanted to see her they could come to Shedog.

'And your conversation might be overheard up there,' Miss Pink observed idly.

Euphemia nodded, and ushered her into the living room where a magnificent range gleamed with blacklead and a kettle was suspended over the fire from a crane like a ship's boom. Above the range was a high shelf with two fine Staffordshire dogs. A brass lamp hung from the ceiling. Euphemia thrust a piece of driftwood under the kettle and gestured to a chair.

'Sit yourself down; we'll have a cup of tea.' Her eyes shifted. 'You think only of your stomach! No one was saying anything about eating!'

A large black cat with a Grecian nose and emerald eyes hurried in making anxious noises. Having made sure that no food was

98

available, he jumped on Miss Pink's lap, kneaded himself into a comfortable position with his arms over her shoulder and went to sleep. The tea was made in a tin pot and placed on the trivet.

Miss Pink said, 'Mrs Hamlyn is going to be lost without your assistance.'

Euphemia looked embarrassed. 'I wouldn't want to hurt Mrs Hamlyn, she knows that.'

'But you don't want everyone to know all your business.'

'I don't know nothing; it's no good keep asking me.'

'Are you afraid of someone?' Miss Pink was blunt.

Euphemia poured the tea. 'Who would I be afraid of?'

'A man who's killed once could very likely kill again, almost certainly to protect himself. If you were out Monday evening and you met someone, on the shore or in the wood, you might keep quiet for fear of getting that person into trouble. But if he was the killer, he'd want to kill you to keep you from talking. If you said what you'd seen, or whom, then you're safe. Do you see?'

'I didn't see nothing,' Euphemia said, bewildered. 'Nothing. The light went out about half past ten and that was all.'

'No one came out of the cottage with a torch? It would be Terry going to wash the dishes in the burn.'

Euphemia was very still. 'I went to sleep, I didn't see nothing. Will you be after telling them that?'

'Yes.' Miss Pink sighed. 'I'll see that everyone knows, then you can come back to the house—can't you?'

'Is Ida Hunt staying?'

'To the best of my knowledge she is.'

'I'll come back then, but remember—' Euphemia was deadly serious, 'I told you everything I know.'

Madge Fraser was packing a small rucksack with food. She had pitched her tent about a hundred yards from the top of the waterfall, not an ideal spot, for the ground was lumpy and would be wet when it rained, moreover at this point the burn was not easily accessible, its banks being miniature rock walls. In fact, the site had appeared abandoned when Miss Pink arrived but within a few moments Madge emerged from a hollow some distance upstream and approached carrying a plastic water bottle. There ensued a search for the top which, being green, took some time to find in the heather. The guide seemed badly organised today.

Miss Pink remarked on the tent which was very different from the sophisticated designs of those on the dunes. The bay front was two triangular flaps fastened with buttons.

'It's old,' Madge explained listlessly. 'The button holes are so worn it comes undone in a breeze but those two loops on the flaps keep it closed. It suits me for the odd occasion. After all,' she added dryly, 'I'm not much interested in clients who can't afford to put me up in a hotel. Can I offer you a cup of tea? I've just had the last of my whisky.'

Miss Pink declined the tea. She glanced at the empty half-bottle on the grass in front of the tent and wondered how often the guide drank whisky in the morning. Aloud she asked, 'Did you go across to Largo on Monday evening?'

'Yes.'

'What did Terry have to say?'

'I didn't see her. I didn't go to the cottage; there was no light.'

'What time was that?'

There was a pause. 'About half past ten.'

'Did you see the light go out?'

'No.'

'Why did you go across if there was no light?'

'There was when I left the house. I looked to see. It went out before I reached the river.' Another pause. 'So I came back.'

'Did you see anyone come out of the cottage?'

'No,' Madge said tightly, 'I didn't see anyone. There was no torch. I came back.' Her tone grated with hostility.

'What time did you return to the house?' Miss Pink wondered why she wasn't told to mind her own business.

'Not long after I turned back. I couldn't have been away for more than ten minutes.'

'What has Vera Hamlyn got against you?'

Madge turned exhausted eyes on the other woman. 'She thinks I'm having an affair with her old man.'

'You quarrelled with her last night?'

'Of course, you were in the passage. Yes, I did. Is it your business?' It was said carelessly, without heat.

Miss Pink looked embarrassed. 'There were two points to clear up: what time the light went out, and the cause of your quarrel with Vera.'

'The light went out around ten-thirty.'

'She was alive some time after that.'

'*What?*' Miss Pink watched with interest as the girl struggled to recover herself. 'Who saw her?'

'Willie MacNeill went to Largo at eleven, at which time she was washing billies in the burn.'

Madge inhaled deeply. It seemed to take a long time for her lungs to fill, then, as she exhaled, she started to giggle quietly. Miss Pink looked at the islands and waited. After a while the giggling stopped and there was a long silence. Far away, probably at Rahane, a dog barked.

'So it was Willie,' came her voice, calmly.

'Willie says she had a man with her.'

'*When?*'

'About eleven,' Miss Pink repeated patiently. She turned and looked at the guide. She had changed—again. Now she was excited. 'I've been such an ass,' she said warmly. 'Lavender was implying the most revolting things about Ken; she was *obscene!* But, well, mud sticks. I got to worrying and remembering things about Ken, and how he was attracted to young girls. Lavender hinted he went over to Largo that night; I think she's getting a kick out of pretending he's the killer.' She took a deep breath. 'Anyway, from about a quarter to eleven until well after midnight he was drinking with me in the lounge.'

Miss Pink nodded. 'That's one point cleared up.'

'I don't think he left that bar all evening. When I came in, he and Gordon were hard at it on one of their interminable arguments.'

'So Hamlyn was there too?'

'Oh yes; the three of us: from before eleven until after midnight.'

Miss Pink looked at her watch. 'I must be getting down.' She hesitated. 'Will you be taking your meals at the house?'

'No, I got some food from the youth hostel. I'm going to do the ridge tomorrow, and I'll be leaving Skye the next day—assuming the police will let me go. Ken's paid me and cancelled the engagement. We couldn't have gone on with it when Lavender was in this mood. I'll fade out and go to the Lakes; my next engagement is in Langdale.'

'Don't you ever take a holiday?'

'When the season's over. Can't afford it before; I've got a daughter, you see.' Miss Pink's face was alert with interest and Madge was forced to elaborate: 'Her father was killed on Monte Rosa before she was born.'

'That was tragic!'

Madge shrugged. 'She might never have known him if he'd lived. He was married and I doubt if he'd have contributed towards her support. He wasn't like that. In any case, I'm making enough to keep a family going. There's my mother too; she's got a widow's pension. She looks after Barbara. We manage all right.' She stood up briskly. 'I'm going to put some grub on the ridge by that Stone Man, and then take the car to Sligachan and leave it to pick up tomorrow evening.'

'How will you get back to Shira today?'

'I'll get a lift; there'll be plenty of people on the road, what with the murder and everything.'

Miss Pink said wonderingly, 'You don't seem to have been affected by Terry's death.'

Madge was surprised at the comment. 'I'm not.' She added earnestly, 'It was bound to happen, you know.'

'But when you said you'd visit her when she was on her own, I thought you liked her.'

'Well, I thought she might be lonely with Colin away. I

mean, she was only a few years older than my kid.'

'But now she's dead, you don't think of her like your own daughter.'

'That's the point! I've got my own people to think about, haven't I? She's gone; what can I do about it?' She was fitting the plastic water bottle into her pack. She glanced up at the headwall of Coire na Banachdich and in an instant she was cool and professional again. 'If the weather breaks, I can always come down the corrie.'

'You think it might be going to break?'

'I don't like it. Something's brewing. The air's sticky. Feel it?'

Chapter 9

'CORROBORATION HELPS.' Merrick indicated the pile of papers in front of him. 'Madge Fraser was with Hamlyn and Maynard in the lounge from a quarter to eleven to ten past midnight because on that point the three of them agree. But there's only her word for it that she turned back from Largo, although several people confirm that the light went out about ten-thirty. Who put it out?'

'I'm beginning to think it was the murderer,' Miss Pink said.

He was puzzled. 'He puts the light out and then helps her wash the dishes? Why put it out when she's still alive?'

'Why does it have to be Terry in the burn?'

'Because he said—wait a minute.' Merrick sorted through the statements, picked one out and read it, his lips moving. He looked up. 'He saw no faces, only torchlight on pans, and he heard only mumbling.' He looked back at the statement. ' "I heard her talking and then I heard a man. . . . I couldn't hear what she said. . . ." So they were both mumbling. I see what you mean, ma'am; he heard a woman and assumed it was Terry, but you think it was another woman—and the killer?'

'Terry was a town girl; would she put the lamp out, wait half an hour, then go outside to wash the pans, and come back to a dark house? I asked Euphemia if someone came out with a torch but she was definite that nothing happened after the lamp was put out. So is Madge Fraser.'

Merrick was dubious. 'Could she have put the lamp out in order to watch *aurora*? She might not have seen the Northern Lights before.'

'It's the time lag,' Miss Pink insisted. 'The lamp went out at ten-thirty, the pans were being washed close to eleven. What was happening during that half hour? I can't believe that Terry was standing outside Largo watching *aurora*.'

'So what do you think was happening? All right, there was a couple washing the pans. Which couple is missing from the house—this house? Or anywhere else,' he added thoughtfully.

'The Lindsays are the only married couple who were both in their rooms at that time,' Ivory said.

Merrick stared at his sergeant. 'Why wash the dishes?' His eyes came round to Miss Pink.

'Billies,' she corrected absently. 'To confuse the issue—the time of death? Irwin wasn't expected back until late the following night. If the murderer left the billies dirty, wouldn't that imply that she died shortly after she'd eaten? But if they were washed, no one would know when she died.'

'It could be more concrete than that,' Merrick said. 'Surely, with MacNeill tipping rubbish, there was a chance she wouldn't be found at all and it would be assumed, since the killer had removed all her belongings—except for that marble chip you found, ma'am—that she'd left the glen? The billies could have been washed to give colour to that theory. If they'd been left dirty, the chances might be that Irwin would suspect foul play simply because, if she'd left him voluntarily, she'd have cleared up first.'

Miss Pink shook her head. 'I doubt if he'd think twice about it. I reckon the killer didn't mind the body being found; all he wanted was to spread the time of death over a few hours because he had no alibi for the actual time.'

There was a pause. 'Read Lindsay's statement,' Merrick said, passing it across. 'See if you can confirm it.'

It was short. 'He doesn't mention that they had a difference of opinion during dinner,' she observed. ' "We left the dining room about seven-thirty...." In fact, he flung out during the pudding course and she hurried after him. I heard them go upstairs. I didn't see them again but then I went up myself about eight-thirty. Does his wife corroborate his statement that they went straight to their room and stayed there until breakfast on Tuesday?'

'I'm sure she will, ma'am.'

'Yes.' She was equally expressionless. 'It will be interesting to learn why they argued so heatedly that evening. She's a powerful woman.'

'Could she carry a body on one of those pack frames?'

'She'd have less difficulty with it than her husband would. I take it you found no unauthorised prints in the Rescue Post?'

He shook his head. Everyone had been fingerprinted for elimination, including herself. 'There were Hamlyn's and the two guides' in the Rescue Post, and only Irwin's and yours in Largo's kitchen.'

She jerked to attention. 'Where were Terry's?'

'Exactly. Largo was wiped after the murder, *and* there were glove smudges. Our chap knows what he's doing. Or our woman. A woman would be more likely to think about washing pans to confuse the time of death. Why would Betty Lindsay want to kill the girl? Because of George Watkins?'

'That's most unlikely. By Monday evening everyone knew how he'd treated Terry; according to Betty, he maintained that the girl was pestering him. She had no reason for killing Terry.'

Merrick leaned back in his chair. 'So if the Lindsays are out of it, who were that pair in the burn? Not the Hamlyns because he was in the bar when the dishes were being washed—the same with Ken Maynard. But the couple in the burn don't have to be married. Madge Fraser admits to being over there, or near there at what we think is the relevant time—'

'I didn't tell you; a curious twist to her account of that incident is that, as I see it, she thought Maynard was the killer; she was hysterical with relief when she learned that the girl was alive at eleven—because she was drinking with Maynard from a quarter to eleven.'

Merrick looked for a statement and found it. 'Maynard says he was with his wife in their room until some time after ten-thirty when he went down to the lounge, then outside ... Why outside? Oh, there was no one behind the bar. "I went back

106

to the cocktail lounge when I heard Hamlyn come downstairs and stayed there until after midnight. Miss Fraser came in at about a quarter to eleven." If that's corroborated by his wife—and we believe her—then he left the house for only a few minutes, and even then he was so close to the front door that he heard Hamlyn come down.'

'What does Hamlyn say on that point?' Miss Pink asked.

'Hamlyn.' He paraphrased: 'He was in the cocktail lounge till just before ten. He had no customers and he went up to his sitting room to listen to the news on the radio, then came down again about ten-thirty. He read his newspaper behind the bar until Maynard and Miss Fraser came in. He went to bed about twelve-fifteen.' He looked up. 'Mrs Hamlyn corroborates his times. She was in their sitting room after dinner. Madge Fraser was with her until about a quarter to ten when the girl went to her room to write a letter.'

'I wonder what they talked about,' Miss Pink mused. 'She must have gone across to Largo about ten-twenty. And that seems to cover everyone in the house. What is Watkins' alibi?'

'I wondered when you were going to come to him. He was drinking at Sligachan. The barman says he was there shortly after seven and stayed until a quarter past ten. He wasn't sober when he left but he appears to have got back to the glen in one piece—which is surprising, considering the shape his old van is in. He could have been in just the right mood to strangle the girl if he found her at his tent, but if he got back before eleven, as he must have done, would the other campers have heard nothing? They've been questioned and no one heard anything out of the way, although they did hear him come back. If he managed to strangle her silently on the camp site, he's still got a hell of a job to get her body to the cliffs, and retrieve all her possessions from Largo. There are two things against it; one, he was too drunk not to leave some trace—and remember, the killer wiped his prints from Largo—and secondly: the times don't fit. If he left Sligachan at ten-fifteen, who put the light out at Largo and who was the man in the burn?'

'He could have been the man in the burn,' Miss Pink protested. 'It takes only twenty minutes or so to drive from Sliga-chan to Glen Shira, but he wouldn't mumble quietly when he was drunk—not George Watkins, and where and when did he have time to pick up the woman he was mumbling with? I agree, it wasn't Watkins—unless something's been missed out.'

'Of course, it's not watertight,' Merrick admitted. 'He didn't have to be drunk. Drunkenness has been simulated before now. And then there's Irwin, with no alibi at all.'

'I didn't think he would have,' Miss Pink said. 'He was in a tent at Sligachan.' She paused. 'I assume it was coincidence that those two were near each other.'

'They didn't meet. Irwin had dinner with his client in the hotel, Watkins was in the public bar. Irwin went to his tent at nine and stayed there until he got up at eight for breakfast. That's his statement, but our local people tell me he had time to get from Sligachan to here and back, without transport, and to dump the body, all during the hours of darkness.'

She thought about that and agreed that it was possible, using the track across the moor, but, she pointed out, there was no shadow of a motive. Like Willie MacNeill, Irwin would never have needed to kill Terry.

Merrick said heavily: 'If we always had to show motive, ma'am, there'd be far fewer convictions.'

'Be that as it may, I like a good sound motive, and so far I don't think you've discovered one. You've gone through the people at Glen Shira House and most of those outside. You're left with the crofters: Captain Hunt and old MacNeill.' Her voice was a little strained. 'I really can't see the Hebridean crofter feeling so passionately about a girl he'd strangle her. I know Hunt is a liar but he's no Dominici.'

'Dominici? Who—? Ah yes. Captain Hunt as a Peeping Tom.' Merrick looked sideways at his sergeant. 'Well, there's a thought. Did that ever occur to you?'

Ivory absorbed it slowly, with a frown.

'And Malcolm MacNeill?' Miss Pink asked. 'I've yet to meet him.' To her astonishment they both looked serious. There was a hint of impatience in her voice: 'Can you see the crofters wiping off prints, washing billies.... Who—' she asked acidly, 'was the woman in the burn? Euphemia?'

Chapter 10

OVER LUNCH THE guests were subdued, discussing, in a desultory fashion, whether it was worth going on the hill for what was left of the day. There was a feeling that Madge had been favoured in being allowed to move out of the house and to go on the ridge, and Miss Pink was in the position of an Aunt Sally at whom questions were fired in attempts to discover what was in Merrick's mind.

She escaped after lunch and strolled down through the trees to the river bank where she paused, ostensibly watching a grey wagtail, but at the same time noting that there was still a uniformed man outside Largo's open door.

The air was heavy and there were high cirrus clouds. In the corries the haze was dissolving so that the peaks crept closer in the hard light, and this sense of movement in a world that should be inanimate was disturbing.

She went left down the river bank and came to a stile over the wall which marked the boundary of the colonel's land. On the other side a plank bridge crossed a burn, and then came the track leading to the camp site. Ida Hunt was coming down the track from the front entrance of Glen Shira House.

'You come the long way round.' Miss Pink stated the obvious.

Ida bit her lip. 'Not much longer.' She added with a rush: 'And 'tis much easier on the road if you're wearing heels.'

Miss Pink's glance passed over the other's sensible sandals but she was old-maidish as she confided: 'I've been having a look at the ground.' In the face of the other's blank look she went on: 'I mean, if he went through the wood. But then that's not the only way of approaching Largo; there's the bridge—which you don't have to use with the river so low—and one might come down the forestry road from the top of the glen. It comes almost as far as Largo. He could have used a car there if the gate at the other end isn't locked.'

'It isn't. Are they thinking he came in from outside—a stranger?'

'Well, not a stranger to her.'

They moved down the track.

'Perhaps someone followed her from London?' Ida ventured. 'Why did they take all our fingerprints then? My man said—' She trailed off, then continued in the same tone, '—they had to look as though they was doing something.'

'And then they had to make sure that no local person had left his prints in Largo.' Ida stared stiffly ahead. 'By "local" I mean everyone who was staying here, of course,' Miss Pink added politely.

Above Rahane's ford they came to Sletta, the Hunts' bungalow. It was new and symmetrical with grass on either side of a pebble path leading to the front door, and two beds of roses suffering from salt and drought.

'Will you come away in?' Ida didn't sound enthusiastic but Miss Pink made up for that deficiency by the eagerness with which she approached the gate.

They went to the front door and Ida turned the handle. Nothing happened and she was embarrassed out of all proportion to the cause.

At the back door they found Captain Hunt sitting on a bench, smoking and contemplating a saw horse. A tiny apricot poodle erupted from behind his thigh boots and flew at its mistress with piercing squeals.

Miss Pink was taken indoors to a spotless sitting room with wall-to-wall carpeting and a view across the camp site to the mountains of Rum. She remarked on the numerous cars parked along the track and the captain told her they belonged to the Press.

'Where are the reporters?' Miss Pink asked.

'They's everywhere, ma'am, and times they collect in one place.... You'll know what a pack of lambs is like all scampering round a field? That's them.' He jerked his head at the camp site. 'Of course,' he added sanctimoniously, 'they's only doing their job. There they go now, see: after Willie.' A string of figures trailed across the dunes behind the tractor. 'He is tipping the rubbish in a hole in the river bank,' the captain explained, 'since they will no' let him tip at Scarf although the body is gone.'

'When was it taken?'

'About midday, ma'am.'

'And how many police are left?'

'There is two in Largo, and one guarding the door makes three. The photographers who took pictures in the geo is gone. There may be one or two poliss on the camp site although Colin and that Watkins has been spoken to.'

'Is Colin Irwin on the camp site?'

'He has put a wee tent on the dunes near Shedog. He will go back to Largo once the poliss is finished there.'

Ida came in with tea, preceded by the neurotic poodle.

'The reporters must get under your feet,' Miss Pink observed.

'Ach no!' the captain said comfortably. 'Silly questions is what you might call an occupational hazard in Glen Shira. Are there people living on the ridge? Is the deer dangerous? How did we get our food before the road was built?'

'Those will not be the questions asked of Watkins, Willie and Irwin.'

He regarded her without expression. 'They can only answer the truth, ma'am—to reporters or poliss. Watkins was drunk, Colin was in his tent at Sligachan.'

'And Willie?'

He was grimly amused as he glanced out of the window where neither reporters nor tractor were to be seen. 'Willie has made his statement and if the newspapermen has got any sense, they'll leave him be.'

Ida turned to her husband. 'The lady says the one who killed the girl could have come down the forestry road in a car.'

He was silent for a moment, assimilating this and studying Miss Pink. 'Ay? He could have. Would the poliss be thinking that, or just yourself, ma'am?'

She ignored the gist of the question. 'When you consider all the approaches, that one must be taken into account.'

'So it could have been a stranger,' Ida told her husband.

A figure passed the window and the poodle indulged in a paroxysm of yapping. It was bundled inside a broom cupboard where it could be heard remotely, working itself into hysterics. Miss Pink followed her hostess to the kitchen as if she were about to take her leave.

An old man with fierce eyebrows, wearing breeches and a deerstalker, came in the back door. It was Malcolm MacNeill, Willie's father.

Edging round the table, Miss Pink beamed at the company and repeated inanely: 'So it could have been a stranger.'

Ida felt forced to explain to the newcomer. 'The lady said that one who killed the girl could have come down the forestry road.'

'Oh ay,' said old MacNeill.

'We've known that all along,' the captain growled. 'It doesna have to be one of us.' He stared at his wife.

A shutter came down over Ida's face. 'It could be anyone,' she agreed.

There was an unnatural silence, then the captain said, 'We had no way of knowing what was going to happen. No one went across there, by daylight.'

'Except Willie.'

'No one to hurt, I mean.'

Miss Pink said silkily, 'Is that what you were thinking yesterday morning when you told me she'd had no visitors and you forgot Willie?'

'I remembered him afterwards. I told the poliss.' None of them was disconcerted, least of all old MacNeill who was standing so that he could see through the doorway and the sitting-room window. He kept shooting glances towards the dunes.

'If a visitor meant harm to her,' Miss Pink mused, 'he wouldn't have gone in daylight.'

'You don't expect murder in Glen Shira,' the captain told her.

Miss Pink raised her eyebrows. 'You don't think she was asking for trouble: the way she dressed?'

The captain said casually, 'We're used to that in the glen; in summer half the campers don't wear clothes, or just half their clothes. Topless, they calls it.'

Old MacNeill said, 'I'm no' worried if they goes mother-naked; 'tis my gates I worries about, and breaking down my fences, but her wasna here long enough to do harm to anyone, poor soul. Willie,' he said with relish, 'is after beating that Watkins to a pulp.'

'Go on!' The captain was grimly pleased.

'He has nearly killed him.'

'Dear knows,' Ida observed, 'but he asked for it.'

'And then he took and rolled the tractor over and over that man's tent until now all the tent and whatever was inside is rolled into the sand and broken.'

'Willie is always fighting over girls,' the captain explained to Miss Pink. 'What shape is the other one in?' he asked of old MacNeill.

'He canna stand up. I doubt they'll be after taking him away to the hospital. I was wondering now would one of you come and help me with my cows?'

There was a flat silence.

'What's wrong with Willie?' the captain asked, too casually.

'Well, now.' Old MacNeill was equally casual. 'I was after thinking they'll be taking him in for assault.'

The others exchanged looks. They seemed remarkably happy. Miss Pink shifted her feet amiably, knowing they were dying for her to leave.

'Young Colin can milk,' the captain said. 'Go down to his tent and take him back with you.'

'A very satisfactory arrangement,' Miss Pink observed. 'He will be company for you, Mr MacNeill.' She glanced across the sitting room. 'But then, he can't be company for Euphemia tonight, can he?' She smiled at them. 'Did none of *you* see or hear anything on Monday night?'

Old MacNeill said, 'I was fast asleep.'

'Our bedroom faces the sea,' the captain told her. 'We didna hear a thing.'

'They're frightened,' Miss Pink maintained. 'They're locking their doors and not sleeping alone.'

She was standing with Merrick on the raised dunes which faced the sea. He had come down from Largo when he learned that Willie was thrashing George Watkins.

'They're all on edge,' he told her. 'That's how I like it; they'll talk better. This assault of Willie's now: gives us justification for taking him in. It's possible he'll find the atmosphere of a police station—when a murder investigation's in progress—a bit more intimidating than his own farmyard.'

'I don't think he did it.'

He raised his eyebrows. 'Whether he did or didn't, I'm hoping he's going to remember a sight more about that night than what he's told us.'

'What the crofters are hoping is that you'll hold him.'

He studied her keenly. 'It needn't mean they think the murderer's still here, you know. Watkins is only going to hospital to be stitched up; he could come back. And Willie attacked Watkins. The fellow was just sitting outside his tent and Willie jumped off his tractor and went for him. The reporters saw it all. And when he'd thrashed the man soundly, he destroyed all his gear.'

'That could have been in return for Watkins' beating Terry; it doesn't mean Willie thinks the man killed her. But the crofters are afraid; why, Ida Hunt won't go through the wood in daylight! And they know everything that goes on, yet on Monday evening they saw and heard nothing. Even if they are ignorant, they must have speculated, but they're as tight as clams. Except when I suggested a stranger might have come to the glen on Monday evening, using the forestry road to approach Largo.'

Merrick was immediately alert. 'He couldn't be a stranger to the glen. . . . A friend of the girl's? But the last anyone outside the glen knew was that she was coming here to join Watkins. How could she have got word out that she'd moved in with Irwin? Only the people in the glen knew that she was alone at Largo that night. Even if anyone outside did know she was at Largo, it would be too much of a coincidence if he also knew that Irwin would be away on Monday night. No, it was an inside job, there's no doubt about that.'

On the site of Watkins' tent, a plainclothes man and a uniformed constable were gingerly retrieving battered objects from the turf. They acknowledged her presence with diffident mumbles but continued with their work. As she stood there, idly wondering whether to return to the house for an early tea or to pay a visit to Shedog, someone gasped, 'Oh, my God!' and Andrew Lindsay blundered past her to stand irresolute behind the constable who was prising a cooking stove out of the sand. Lindsay turned horrified and appealing eyes on Miss Pink.

'Did you see what he did to him! He nearly killed him! He can't walk! They had to bring him up to the house by car, and now they've taken him to hospital. He's a *hospital* case!'

The detective was listening avidly and the uniformed man was merely making motions with his hands but Lindsay wouldn't have been concerned if they'd been recording him.

Miss Pink said soothingly, 'Perhaps there was some resentment between them; it could have cleared the air.'

There was a prolonged silence after this inanity. The police made meaningless passes over the chaos in the turf and the horror died in Lindsay's face.

'I see,' he said at last and sulkily. 'You think it was over the girl. Jealousy.' His eyes blazed again. 'What? He thinks George killed her?' Miss Pink had said nothing and now, dreading the moment when he would dry up in the presence of the Law, she moved away. He followed, clutching at her sleeve. 'But that's mad! George was over at Sligachan; he got drunk that night. In any case, he didn't care who she went to; it was all over between them.' He walked on with bowed head, absently kicking the daisies. After a while he continued unpleasantly, 'This hasn't done MacNeill any good, just the opposite: it's clinched the case against him. They've taken him in; he'll be charged with assault.' His voice was rising again. 'George—' he choked on the name, '—he's lost several teeth ... they might have gone down his throat—he could have killed him!'

She did not voice her private thoughts on that but sat down on a dry bank facing the sea. This put her in mind of Watkins sitting beside her above Eas Mor yesterday. Some of these people were incapable of dissimulation when they were disturbed. She asked gently, 'Would George have minded if Terry had been pregnant?'

'He wouldn't have cared,' he responded flatly. 'She could never have proved it. She was a tart. But she wasn't pregnant.'

'Difficult to tell,' she murmured.

'She didn't look pregnant,' he insisted. 'No, she couldn't have been.'

'You must have been watching her through binoculars,' she said pleasantly.

He glared at her. 'Why the hell—? I never watched her. Why should I? I'm not—I wasn't interested in her!'

'How many times did you meet her?'

'I never met her.'

'You met her on Saturday evening; you may not have been introduced, perhaps you didn't speak to her, but you were standing right next—'

'That was the only time; I never saw her again.'

'You must have done because in the dress she wore that evening you couldn't have sworn she wasn't pregnant, and you're so certain. It was the style of dress women might wear when they *are* pregnant.'

His eyes wandered. 'I didn't see her again.'

'So Betty did.'

He licked his lips and looked crafty. 'Yes,' he agreed carelessly, 'Betty saw her again.'

'When?' She caught a flicker in his eyes. 'You were on the White Slab the day that Irwin left, and that evening you quarrelled with your wife and left the dining room quickly. Where did Betty go?'

He grinned at her. 'You'd better ask her. *I* stayed in the bedroom.'

The air was thickening over Loch Shira, forming a belt of sea fog, and at the same time the corries were filling with an opaque but brilliant mist which seemed to seep like steam out of cracks in the rocks.

As Miss Pink strolled towards the big house, these isolated patches of vapour spread and coalesced, the belt behind her moved landward, but for a few minutes the peaks stood above it, violet-coloured and appearing incredibly high.

By the time she reached the house the atmosphere was dim and clammy. The front door was open to the fog and the place appeared empty. She walked round to the back. She had not been here before but was not surprised that there should be no sign of the squalor usually found at the rear of catering establishments. The Hamlyns' Avenger and an old but gleaming Rescue Land Rover were parked neatly in the yard. There were no empty beer crates, no over-flowing dustbins, in fact, but for the iron fire escape, it could have been the back of a private residence, and even the fire escape might have been the work of a responsible paterfamilias.

There was a movement inside a stable and Hamlyn appeared in the doorway, critically inspecting a helmet. His surprise at her presence was superseded by a different kind of alertness as he cocked an eye at the wraiths of fog drifting through the trees.

'Now what does this mean?' It was a rhetorical question. 'Sea fog. Heat? But the forecast is "unsettled". However, I don't think it'll come to much.'

'That's just as well, with Madge hoping to traverse the ridge tomorrow.' She was examining a cushion of stonecrop in the stones of the mounting block. 'Wall pepper,' she observed. 'It must like the lime in the mortar. Surely these buildings aren't of limestone?'

'Granite—from the Red Hills. She's going to do the ridge tomorrow?'

'So she says. I would think it will be more difficult in cloud.'

'Not for someone who knows the way. I've done it in cloud.'

'Indeed. You must have been a very active man in your prime. You'd leave most of your contemporaries behind even now.'

He made a deprecating gesture but it was at variance with his tone. 'Four principles: a good diet, plenty of exercise and fresh air, and positive thinking. It's as simple as that.' She beamed and nodded. 'But you subscribe to that philosophy yourself,' he pointed out as if accusing her.

'As fully as I can.' She peered inside the stable. 'Are you restoring order? Can I see the equipment?'

'Certainly.' He stood back and motioned her inside.

She looked with interest at the paraphernalia of rescue: rucksacks, pack frames, radio sets, a pile of plastic bags. Below a wall map was a telephone and clipboard, and three stretchers were suspended from beams by an ingenious system of pulleys. It looked very professional.

'It's fascinating to see how different people organise a Post,' she admitted. 'Tell me—' her hand rested on a shelf but now she lifted it with a look of horror. 'I shouldn't have done that,' she murmured, 'I've left a print.'

'The police have finished in here; that's how I come to be replacing the stuff. They've gone over the place with a tooth comb but they've come up with nothing that shouldn't be here. I understand the same thing's happened with personal pack frames. Only four of us have them: the guides, Irwin and myself.'

'But the frames will be covered with their owners' prints.'

'Well.' He coughed in deference to the gentler sex. 'They were looking for traces, d'you see, hairs and things.'

She considered this and then remarked that a survival bag was concerned too. He looked guilty.

'I'm naughty about inventories; there could be a bag missing, I can't be certain. But the police seemed sure that there were no strange prints in here. However, I suppose he could have worn gloves?'

'Glove prints will show.'

'Is that so? Intriguing, this fingerprint business. Did you have yours taken?'

'Oh yes.'

He was sly. 'So even you are a suspect, ma'am.'

'Possibly, but I would think they took them for elimination purposes. I was at Largo, you see.'

'You were? When?'

'Yesterday morning.'

'Of course. I was wondering if you'd gone across the previous night.'

'No.' She regarded him levelly. 'When I said goodnight to you on Monday evening, I was on my way to bed.'

He clapped a hand to his forehead with a theatrical gesture. 'People's movements! I'm starting to act like a detective myself! They keep asking me where everyone was, as if I were a kind of spider at the centre of a web. I know where they are when they're in the cocktail lounge, that's all.'

She smiled in sympathy. 'Did you know that Willie MacNeill had gone to the police station?'

It took him a moment to assimilate this. 'Did he go voluntarily?'

'No. He assaulted Watkins.'

He sighed in exasperation. 'I told you so: only yesterday. No discipline, you see, no self-control; all these closed communities are the same; they were all right while the old values held and the community had leaders for whom—'

'Colonel!' He stopped in mid-flight and gaped at her. 'Forget about Glen Shira for a moment,' she ordered sternly, 'George Watkins comes from an urban environment but he had considerably less control. The only way he could end a relationship he found unsatisfactory was to use violence. Willie's thrashing Watkins was perfectly natural; I don't blame him a bit.'

'Ha!' He'd recovered and was jovial although he didn't look amused. 'You approve of primitive instincts?' He shook his head seriously. 'But we can't have it in a civilised community, d'you see. They make the mistake of thinking of freedom as licence, but freedom carries obligations; even animals are very highly organised.' He smiled at her. 'We can't have people taking the law into their own hands, that's anarchy. What I always say is: it doesn't matter what you do so long as you don't hurt anyone. Now I admit that sounds like licence but you think about it, dear lady, you think!'

'Generalisations can be dangerous,' she murmured.

He hardly heard her. 'There is nothing you can do that doesn't affect someone else—unless you're stuck on a desert island. We're all interdependent, and in a place like this any lack of consideration sticks out like a sore thumb. It isn't just bad manners then; it becomes anti-social behaviour. Look at that tip in Scarf Geo! There are dead sheep down there, ma'am! That's illegal. But, as you say, it's not only the crofters—' he looked startled. 'In fact, they may not be so bad; it's possible I've been doing them an injustice. The visitors are city folk: marginally better educated perhaps, but look at them: transistors on the shore, stealing produce from the garden, lighting fires in the woods—' his eyes became more protuberant. 'You have the same situation in Cornwall; the police have a load of trouble with artists and drugs in St Ives.'

'Britain is such a small country; there's so little room for people to enjoy—'

'There are too many people!'

She divined what was coming and edged towards the door. He raised his voice in an effort to detain her: 'The fact is that the lower their intelligence, the more prolific they are, and in poor Catholic countries you see it at its worst. Look at Ireland! This modern emphasis on population control: two children to every family! It's suicidal! D'you know what will happen? The middle classes will limit their numbers and the masses will breed like rabbits—and in a few generations they'll have bred us out of existence!'

Miss Pink said weakly, 'So what do you suggest?'

Suddenly he looked tired and old, and ashamed. 'It's the crunch, isn't it? And I talk about positive thinking!' He was obviously suffering. 'I'm glad we had no children. What would it be like for our grandchildren? Have you seen a pop concert on television?' His tone was flat. 'The audience isn't even adolescent; they are *little* girls. And they're the future mothers of the race. And when you see those ... those *animals* posturing on the stage, manipulating them....' He stared at her. He was breathing heavily. 'That is not decadence, ma'am, the decadence lies in the people manipulating the puppets. We have reached the stage of free bread and circuses, d'you see?' Suddenly he gave a boyish grin. 'They'll be putting drugs in the drinking water next. Of course, we've got our own supply.' It was self-parody and Miss Pink smiled faintly.

'What can you do?' he asked pleasantly. 'What do *you* do?'

'Me? Oh, I cultivate my garden. I'm self-sufficient for vegetables and fruit; I keep bees....'

'Drop in the ocean,' he said, following her into the yard. 'When you hear that louts have put a girder on the line in front of an express train, I suppose you go out and transplant the lettuces?'

'As a matter of fact, I do.'

Chapter 11

AT FIVE MINUTES to six the weather forecast was still unsettled and Miss Pink regarded the gloom outside her windows with scepticism. It looked like a November evening and she could no longer see Largo. At six o'clock she smelt peat smoke and went downstairs to find that the fires had been lit.

Maynard was in the cocktail lounge, and Hamlyn behind the bar. Maynard had been for a row in Captain Hunt's dinghy but, seeing the fog coming in, he'd retreated hastily and had been invited to take a dram with the captain. Thus he had heard about the fracas on the camp site although his version had it that Watkins was in custody too. At this point Hamlyn remarked that the glen would be a better place for the loss of its trouble makers. Maynard stared at him.

'If neither young MacNeill nor Watkins is the murderer,' he observed, 'then the worst trouble maker—' he stressed the words ironically, '—is still here. He could be one of us.'

Hamlyn gaped at him then turned for help to Miss Pink. Maynard, enjoying his host's consternation, said, 'Right, so it isn't Watkins or Willie. Let's say, excluding the hostel people —and I reckon we do : they're outwith our cosy little community —there are—' he lapsed into a mumbled calculation on his fingers while Hamlyn glared belligerently, '—it leaves six men unaccounted for.'

His listeners' eyes glazed predictably. Miss Pink responded first, 'That is correct, but only if you include the crofters.'

'Which you don't,' Maynard said easily. 'No motive. So excluding them, you're left with Lindsay, Irwin, me—' he smiled gaily at Hamlyn, '—and you.'

123

Hamlyn said, 'What motive did I have?'

'Oh, sex.' The other's tone was earnest. 'It was a sex crime.'

Betty Lindsay came in wearing a khaki safari suit which made her look like a navvy. As he turned from Hamlyn, Miss Pink saw that Maynard was not really amused. Tonight his baiting of the colonel was a defence mechanism.

'And there is Betty,' he remarked outrageously, 'who is as strong as a man.'

She was preoccupied. 'What's that, sweetie?'

'You're a likely candidate for the killer.'

'Really? I'll have a large gin, Gordon. Why me?' she continued, folding a pound note and tapping it on the bar.

'Why anyone?' Maynard lost interest and turned to Miss Pink. 'I'm going on the hill tomorrow, no matter what the police say. I've only got two more days and I'm not staying down in the glen for another of them. This place gives me the willies. Will you come out with me?'

'I should like that. Madge is hoping to do the ridge and I'd enjoy seeing her go past. From the right spot we should be able to watch her for a long way.'

'I'll come with you,' Betty put in.

. Ken blinked but his tone was pleasant. 'We'll make up a party then. Where do you suggest we go?'

'I think we should go to Mhic Coinnich or Alasdair,' Miss Pink said. 'She's cached some food on Banachdich so, to encourage her, we ought to meet her halfway between the start, at Gars Bheinn, and the cache.'

'The start is her tent,' Maynard said.

'What's a cache?' Betty asked.

'Some food and water; she's put it under a stone on the Banachdich pass.'

'I hope she can find it again,' Hamlyn said.

'There's an obvious perched block on the north side of the pass with a hole about six feet from its base. She could come straight down to her tent from there if she decided for some reason not to continue.'

'Will she be in for dinner?' Betty asked innocently. Apparently she knew nothing of the under-currents in the house. The men remained silent and Hamlyn busied himself with a glass cloth.

'I doubt it,' Miss Pink said. 'She'll be up before dawn so I expect she'll have an early night.'

Betty glanced at Maynard suspiciously. She would be remembering that his engagement with Madge had two days to run but she didn't comment. Instead she said loudly, 'That's fixed then—for tomorrow? But how are we going to find her if this doesn't clear?' She gestured towards the window.

'It'll clear,' Hamlyn told her. 'It's only a sea fog.'

Andrew Lindsay slouched into the room. His eyes were rimmed with red and he ordered a large whisky without speaking to any of the guests. Betty exclaimed brightly, 'I must go and put things together,' and left the bar. Maynard made nervous grimaces and eyed Miss Pink.

'Where is Lavender?' she asked with a sinking heart, dreading that she might be contributing to the tension.

'Not feeling too good; she won't be down for dinner.'

Hamlyn looked concerned. 'Can we do anything? Broth, toast ... She must have something.'

'I'll ask her later. She had some toast at tea time.'

Dinner was a silent meal with the Lindsays hardly speaking to each other, and Miss Pink and Maynard alone at their tables. Afterwards, Lindsay went out in the grounds and the others drifted back to the lounge to find a coffee tray on the table in the window but no one behind the bar.

'I'm for brandy,' Betty announced truculently. 'Miss Pink, what can I get you?'

'A Cointreau, please.'

'Ken?'

'Brandy, dear.' He spoke absently. He stood in the window, jingling coins in his pocket and staring at the fog.

Betty rang the bell on the counter. The door behind the bar opened and Euphemia looked in. 'Yes, miss?'

'Oh, it's you!' In her surprise Betty sounded rude. 'We want drinks.'

'Mrs Hamlyn's upstairs in their sitting room.'

'Well, where's the colonel?'

'In the stable. Will I be after fetching him?'

'If you will.'

Euphemia backed out. Two minutes later Hamlyn bustled in.

'So sorry,' he breathed, 'didn't think you'd finish so soon. I'm trying to get the rescue equipment sorted.'

'If you'll just attend to us, you can go back to it.' Betty's tone was acid and Maynard raised expressive eyebrows at Miss Pink. The sarcasm failed to rile Hamlyn.

'Not at all,' he countered comfortably. 'While my guests are in the bar, I'm here to serve them. There's plenty of time for the gear.'

'It's just this kind of weather you might have an accident,' Betty pointed out, still unpleasantly, but he didn't respond, merely served their drinks with the deft movements of a barman.

After a while Andrew Lindsay came in from the hall, stood at the bar making desultory conversation with Hamlyn, then drifted out again. Vera put her head round the door, smiled at the guests and asked her husband who was in the stable.

'No one. Why?'

'The light's on.'

'Yes, I left it on. I was working out there.'

Maynard was at the bar now. 'Serve this round,' he told the other firmly, 'and go out and finish it. We can spare you.'

'I'll relieve you as soon as we're finished in the kitchen,' Vera promised. 'Give me a quarter of an hour.'

Betty excused herself, saying she was going to write letters. Hamlyn went away and Maynard and Miss Pink were left alone.

'We're all very restless,' he observed.

'How is Lavender?'

'She's feeling better now; she's had some toast and chicken broth.' Miss Pink didn't comment. 'We all have our drugs,' he said, and downed his brandy at a gulp. 'Lavender's is ill-health. And now I've finished my drink, do I wait to be served? Like hell I do.' He got up and went behind the bar to pour himself a Martell. He returned to his seat.

'Brandy isn't your drug,' Miss Pink said thoughtfully.

'No.' His mouth twitched but he didn't smile. 'This is a superficial palliative ... but not for a superficial sorrow, would you say?' He slumped in his chair. 'No, you wouldn't. She was beautiful and young and innocent but she was nothing to do with me; I didn't even want to go across to Largo. The tragedy is: I don't care.'

'Why are you drinking then?'

'Because of that. I'm burned out. Because a beautiful being has been wantonly destroyed and all I'm concerned about is that I've missed a day's climbing.'

'Why do you think the murder was wanton?'

'Surely the destruction of beauty is always that?'

'Not necessarily. There could have been a good reason for killing her.'

He opened his mouth to reply but at that moment Vera Hamlyn came in. She glanced round the bar in rueful concern at its emptiness, then poured herself a gin. Maynard stood up.

'You can't stay behind the bar, dear; come and join us.'

'Well—'

'Do come, Mrs Hamlyn.' Miss Pink added her persuasion.

Vera came across. 'I'll draw these curtains then; it's such a miserable night.' She looked round the lounge again. 'How quiet we are,' she said, and shivered.

'The nights are drawing in,' Miss Pink observed, and thought how tired the other looked.

'It's been an exhausting day, what with the police—and everything.'

'Why do you think she was killed?' Maynard asked of Miss Pink. Vera stared at him, blinked, and transferred her gaze to the older woman who made a helpless gesture.

'Who can tell? We've been speculating since yesterday. Quite frankly, I'm drained of ideas and prefer to stick to facts. It seems obvious that she was strangled, and most probably at

Largo; those aren't facts but they'll do until we know the results of the autopsy.'

'When will that be?' Vera asked.

'I believe a pathologist was arriving today. We should know tomorrow.'

Vera said, 'Did you get any joy from the crofters?' Miss Pink was startled and the other smiled wryly. 'Euphemia has put herself on the pay-roll again; she said you were at Sletta.'

'And me?' Maynard asked.

'You went rowing before the fog came in, then had half an hour at Sletta.'

'Good God!' He grinned nastily. 'The fog will stop them; they can't see through that.'

'Don't you believe it; they say news runs through the grass in Glen Shira.' For the second time she shivered.

Miss Pink appeared to be following her own line of thought, sparked off by an earlier question. 'I don't think the crofters care enough.'

'To kill,' Maynard elaborated.

'Someone cared.' Vera said. 'A lover presumably.'

'A former lover?' Maynard hazarded. 'One who never made it? A young man on the make, a middle-aged roué obstructed, or old age killing what it hated?'

Vera frowned. 'Is that brandy, Ken?'

'Yes, dear; a double, please.'

'Are you climbing tomorrow?'

He hesitated. 'Yes.' There was a pause. 'I'm going to cheer Madge along the ridge.'

His glass wasn't empty but Vera picked it up and went to the bar.

'Your friend,' he emphasised, following her. Miss Pink sat like a cat by a mouse hole. He put both hands on the counter. 'Your friend Madge,' he repeated.

'I think you should go to bed after this one.' Vera put his glass on the counter. She was a bad colour under her tan.

'You know you're in the wrong, don't you?' he told her earnestly.

'I'm not talking about it.' Her voice was rising.

He snorted derision. 'Gordon and Madge! Don't give me that!'

'You're being impertinent—'

'You're *fond* of her! What's she done that you suddenly—' He stopped as if switched off and the silence drew out agonisingly. Miss Pink watched his rigid back and, in the mirror, his staring eyes, and Vera's eyes, not staring but watching carefully, flicking towards the window and back to Maynard.

'Oh no,' he breathed. 'Not Madge! You're mad, you're off your—' He turned and looked at Miss Pink. With great care he pulled himself together. It was a long process, then, 'I am most appallingly drunk,' he announced. 'Please accept my apologies.'

Leaving his brandy on the counter, he walked out of the room and up the stairs.

In the taut silence Vera fidgeted with something below the counter. Miss Pink was wondering how to re-open the conversation, if that were possible, when she was spared the decision by the return of Hamlyn, breathing satisfaction.

'One thing I'll say for this—event; it's made me introduce some order into that stable.'

'Anything you have to do with is always in apple-pie order.' Vera sounded like an automaton.

'That's only the appearance. Anyone can make a neat stack on a shelf, but the shelves themselves were filthy! It's a good job all the First Aid stuff is sealed—by Jove, yes!' He chuckled. 'Not that sterile equipment makes any difference in practice. Jimmie Carr always says he'd sooner operate in an open field than in an operating theatre.'

'Why?' Miss Pink asked, because someone had to say something.

'Bugs in the air conditioning!' As he roared with laughter Vera slipped out through the kitchen door.

It rained in the night and although this cleared the sea fog, in the morning clouds were skimming the watershed on the western side of the glen. Largo was closed and abandoned and Miss Pink wondered who would be the next person to occupy it—or would old MacNeill let it crumble into ruin?

As she came downstairs Betty Lindsay was leaving the dining room. The woman looked as if she hadn't slept much and she explained, rather long-windedly, that Lindsay had taken Watkins' van to the hospital, so now she must go over in their car to bring her husband back. Miss Pink was puzzled. It seemed early for Watkins to have rung Glen Shira, but Betty's expression was defiant. It might be advisable to wait until evening before asking for elucidation.

Maynard was alone in the dining room, drinking black coffee. He regarded her guiltily. 'Please don't say anything,' he implored, 'I'm far too ill.'

She glanced at the window. 'Perhaps some fresh air—?'

'I might be able to crawl uphill. At least Betty isn't coming.'

'Have you seen the police?'

'No, and I don't intend to. They don't seem to have left anyone in the glen last night, so let's get away before they arrive.'

Miss Pink, who had her own reasons for wanting to talk to him in private, agreed and, against her principles, hurried over her breakfast. It was raining again by the time they were ready to leave but they didn't hesitate and started smartly up the drive in their waterproofs, speculating on whether Madge would retreat, go on regardless, or shelter under a rock. Maynard thought she would shelter; she wasn't out for a record and she would not want to continue the traverse in wet clothes. She would be travelling light and carrying no waterproofs.

'Aren't we being remiss in not backing her better?' Miss Pink asked. 'Surely people doing the ridge normally have more support?'

'Not nowadays, not chaps, anyway; they just pop out and do it, and Madge wouldn't expect any discrimination in her favour. I did think of going up last night to wish her well and ask if there was anything we could do, but by the time I'd thought about it, it was too late.'

Miss Pink remembered the state he was in. 'And one wouldn't want to be wandering around in the dark and fog on the lip of this ravine.'

'Good Lord, no!'

The fall was in view with quite a lot of water going over the drop and looking most dramatic against the green foliage and purple heather. Then Madge's tent appeared but there was no one moving around it. Still higher, they looked back because it faced upstream, but the flaps were closed, which indicated that she was on the ridge ahead of them, as they'd expected.

'What time would she start?' Miss Pink asked.

'About five. I'm going like a cripple. Don't you think it would be best to go straight up the Sgumain Stone Shoot? If we did a route to reach the ridge, she could go along the top while we were climbing and we'd miss her. If we go up the Sgumain screes we could be on Alasdair quickly.'

'Scree!' she repeated feelingly.

He had his way, not least because all the steep rock looked dauntingly wet and cold in the cloud shadow. The Sgumain screes were strenuous but they were safe.

It was also eerie. They scrambled upwards into mist and the black rock walls closed round them. It was far too warm but by the time they stepped out on the summit ridge, the rain had stopped and they could take off their stifling waterproofs. Anoraks followed, and as they started off again, with big loads but in their shirtsleeves, there was a hint of blue above, a glimpse of a dark loch far below and next time Miss Pink looked up all the peaks to the south were rampant against a cerulean sky.

'If it's been like this since dawn,' Maynard said, 'she'll be a fair way along the ridge already.'

'She won't be this far. What a pity we can see only the peaks; she must be in sight at this moment, or would be if the cloud would drop a little more.'

They avoided the Bad Step of Alasdair by an easy chimney and were on the summit by one o'clock, still with no sign of the guide, but they were not too surprised at this. Only the top hundred feet or so of the highest peaks were clear of the cloud; for long stretches the ridge was invisible. They settled down with rocks as back-rests and ate their lunch. It was strange that no one should appear at all; they assumed that the climbers were still climbing and that scramblers wouldn't venture on the ridge when they thought that it was in cloud. They did see people on the Inaccessible Pinnacle across Coire Lagan but they were going the wrong way: north to south. Madge would be moving north.

At last Maynard said, 'I can remember mentioning Madge last night but what did I *say*?'

'You told Vera that an affair between Hamlyn and Madge was ridiculous.'

'So it is.' There was another silence. After a while he asked carelessly, 'Was there anything else?'

'There was a suggestion that Madge killed Terry; that Vera could have suspected that.'

'How circumspect. I didn't actually accuse Vera of harbouring that suspicion?'

'No. And she knew you were drunk.'

'It's fortunate that I should have made an exhibition of myself in front of the only two people who won't spread it around.'

'That could have been deliberate.'

'You mean, I *chose* you?'

'Or you didn't mind getting drunk in our presence. You had to let off steam.'

He stared at the mist wafting round the stolid bulk of Mhic Coinnich across an enormous chasm. 'It was missing this that was the trouble,' he said quietly, 'and losing Madge.' After a while he added, 'There's nothing between us. You're not surprised. I think you know what I'm talking about.'

'And there's your magazine.'

'How discerning of you. You're so right: no one can exploit sex if they still have any passion left. Funny, I took over that publication with such high principles—but that was before the deluge.... One only has so much energy, and if one's lived

a riotous—and perhaps careless—life, the privileges one's en-
joyed spawn responsibilities; like dragons' teeth, of course.' He
turned his spaniel eyes on her. 'One can't disown mistakes and
if you can't remedy them you have to learn to live with them.
Marrying was a mistake.' He did not qualify that by suggesting
that he might have married someone other than Lavender and
then it wouldn't have been a mistake. 'And a few years ago,'
he went on, 'there was Madge, after others. The others didn't
matter; they were just lovely girls. Madge was hardly a gorgeous
mistress but I needed her as much for what she represented as
what she was. After all, we fall in love with an ideal, don't
we? It's all subjective. She was rather dull on a weekend in
London, but a fortnight with her on Skye—and twice we went
to the Alps—these times were out of this world. For the routes
we did, of course; you've got that? Our affair was so short-lived
and innocuous compared with—a kind of triangular relationship: rock, Madge, me, that it hardly mattered. It would have
died and we'd have gone on as a climbing team, but Lavender
found out. You can imagine the result.'

Miss Pink stirred uncomfortably but said nothing. There
was no need to. She had known Lavender for five days.

He went on, 'Lavender is alone in the world. She's only got
me. On the other hand she can make life pretty unbearable.
There's been blackmail on both sides. Now I am "allowed"
Madge for two holidays a year and some weekends but, of
course, even if I loved her, there'd be no affair, not after Lavender discovered it. There are more ways than one of emasculating
a man.'

Miss Pink thought for a moment, not offering facile sympathy,
then she said, 'I think she is more jealous in these circumstances.'

'Naturally. She could never have competed in the same field.
If it's only a matter of sex, women can blame their inadequacy
on age or loss of looks—there's always some alibi, something
they can share with other ageing women. What Lavender finds
literally unbearable is that I go to Madge not for bed but to
be taken up steep rock.'

'And she knows you enjoy rock more than sex,' Miss Pink pointed out. 'It's logical.'

After a while he said quietly, like a child, 'These don't hurt you,' meaning the mountains.

'Well—'

'There's no malice,' he amended. Suddenly he looked round, startled. 'But where is she? And what's happened to the weather?'

Insidiously but very fast, the sky had been overdrawn by an opaque film. A breeze came sniffing round the rocks like a dog with a wet nose.

'She must have passed Alasdair before we got here,' he said. 'At that rate she'll be going up Dearg now, and there's the cloud....'

Miss Pink raised her binoculars. 'There's a party coming down the side of the Inaccessible under the South Crack, but they're three, and going the wrong way. We won't see a thing now; the cloud's rising faster than a climber.'

'It's only two o'clock; shall we follow her route round the skyline?'

They set off but had hardly reached the top of the next point when they were engulfed by the cloud and navigation became tricky. They didn't speak and they forgot the guide; they needed all their concentration for their footing. As Mhic Coinnich loomed above, Miss Pink felt a prickling sensation on her scalp and saw that her companion's hair was standing on end.

'There's too much electricity about,' she called. 'Let's get off the ridge.'

They were close to the easy descent into Coire Lagan but they'd lost only a few hundred feet of height when the storm struck and further progress was accompanied by glaring flashes and stupendous claps of thunder which rolled and reverberated through all the corries. Then the rain came, hissing across the dry rocks and then settling to a dull drumming on their heads like small rubber balls.

'She'll have to come off now,' Miss Pink said, and he nodded.

'She'll come down Coire Banachdich.'

But the storm didn't last long and by the time they came to the mouth of Coire Lagan the clouds were clearing, and again the peaks stood gaunt and dry above the steaming corries.

The tent came into view across the burn but no one moved about it and the flaps were still closed. They studied the back of Coire na Banachdich through binoculars but could see no sign of her, so they assumed that she was continuing the traverse of the ridge.

Below the tent they looked back at the fall and noticed that there was less water in it than there had been this morning. So what they'd seen then must have been last night's rain running off; the recent storm would make little, if any difference to the level of the burns.

Miss Pink bathed and then made tea in her room. She was enjoying her second cup when there was a knock at her door. Betty entered, wearing the same khaki suit she'd worn last night and at breakfast, so crumpled now that she might have slept in it. She looked exhausted.

Miss Pink glanced at her and immediately filled a second cup with tea, then she got up to fetch her medicinal brandy.

'Andy's gone,' Betty said without passion. 'He's cleared off with George Watkins. They've eloped.'

She started to laugh stridently.

Chapter 12

'H E L E F T A note,' Betty explained, gulping brandy from a
bathroom tumbler, 'saying George had rung telling him to take
the van to the hospital. Of course, no one had rung; I asked
the Hamlyns. The note was on the dressing table when I came
upstairs last night. And then I realised that Andy had taken all
his things. I didn't get too excited about that. We had a row on
Monday, you may have noticed; he slammed out of the dining
room. I'd been putting the pressure on; there's this house for
sale outside Portree: a bargain, and I wanted to put a deposit
on it. He wasn't having any, put his foot down, refused to leave
the south.... You know how one thing can lead to another?'
Miss Pink nodded sympathetically. 'In the end—upstairs—we
were quarrelling about George. That was nasty. The atmosphere's been tense for the last few days. So last night I wasn't
really surprised when I saw he'd gone—' she smiled wryly,
'—after all, he had left me the car; I went down to check.
Funny thing, it didn't seem significant at the time that he'd
taken George's van. I thought he'd spend the night in Broadford
or somewhere and then ring me to go and pick him up. He
didn't ring so I went over this morning. When I got to the
hospital they told me Andy called some time after nine last
night. George had been waiting for him. Then one of the
ambulance men said he'd seen them go to a hotel in the village
so I went and looked in the register. They'd left, of course, but
they'd signed in: under a false name, Drummond, and shared
a room.'

'Cheaper,' Miss Pink murmured.

One side of Betty's mouth rose. 'I've known all along; I refused to acknowledge it, even to myself. You can keep up a better front that way.'

Miss Pink nodded surprised approval. 'But,' she pointed out, 'flight looks very suspicious at this moment.'

'No one's been told not to go.' She was on the defensive and Miss Pink realised she was still fighting for this strange couple.

'Perhaps Merrick was hoping something like this would happen,' she mused. 'I thought it curious that they should have left us to ourselves last night.'

'You mean, he expected George and Andy to—to—'

'He might have been expecting someone to make a run for it.'

'Well, it won't worry them. George will be amused at being hunted by the police. He's probably making a game of it right now. He won't have much success though; he hasn't got the brain for a criminal.'

'You don't seem to have any illusions left.'

'I never had. He's a mutton-headed oaf, and I'm not the first woman to be attracted to one.' She stared at the other belligerently.

'Is that why you went to Largo on Monday evening: because you wanted to catch him with Terry and have a show-down?'

Betty's mouth hung open. After a moment she gasped, 'How did you find that out?' Miss Pink sighed. 'I see,' the other continued flatly, 'Andy told you.'

'It wasn't calculated malice. He'd mentioned that Terry was "flat as a board" when pregnancy was referred to, you remember? So I thought he must have met her after Saturday evening because then her dress was concealing—in that respect. Someone must have seen her in other clothes, or through binoculars from the house—which didn't sound like your husband.' Miss Pink was poker-faced. 'Nor,' she added more naturally, 'like you. It seemed more likely that you had gone to Largo, and then told him.'

Betty was deflated. After a moment she remembered the original question. 'Yes,' she admitted, 'I did go across because I thought she'd be with someone; perhaps I hoped it would be George. I was in a horrible mood; I felt that a violent confrontation, particularly with George, was what I needed at that moment.'

'And was she alone?'

'Yes. I didn't go in. There were no curtains, or they weren't drawn. I watched her for a while and then I came away.'

'Did you get the impression that she was quite alone? Could there have been a visitor anywhere else? Upstairs, for instance, or even outside?'

Betty stared. 'I wouldn't think so. If there was, she didn't know it. She was reading, and then she got up and hefted the kettle so I came away quickly in case she came outside for water. I didn't want her to catch me there. By that time I felt awful. I saw the bruises on her face and I felt like a Peeping Tom.'

'What was the time?'

'Not late; about nine.'

'Did you hear anyone on your way back—or at any time while you were out?'

'No, but I was too early; she must have been killed after eleven. Willie saw her alive then.'

Miss Pink looked blank. 'But that may have had no particular relevance to when her killer went across, you see.'

'You mean he may have gone there much earlier than eleven.' She leaned back in Miss Pink's easy chair. She was a better colour now as her rather slow brain started to follow the line which was appearing to her. She looked up quickly to find herself observed. 'You're thinking I was powerful enough to carry her body to Scarf Geo. Quite true. I didn't do it though.' Miss Pink nodded with a small neutral smile. 'The field's pretty limited now, isn't it?' Betty was thoughtful. 'Obviously it wasn't George or Andy. *You* may include them but I know it wasn't. So that leaves Ken, Gordon Hamlyn, Colin Irwin. Who else? The crofters?'

Miss Pink said, 'I think we ought to dress.'

Betty appeared not to have heard her. 'Isn't that odd,' she murmured, 'Madge and Vera are just as strong as me.' She stared at Miss Pink in horror. 'Madge *and* Vera? Why has Madge gone up to the waterfall? Do you know?' Miss Pink stood up and smoothed her bed. Betty stood too. 'The service stairs are down this passage,' she said, 'after the Hamlyns' suite; they've got a sitting room and bedroom farther along. And then there's the ·fire escape; anyone could go and come secretly. Madge is on this corridor too. How did she appear today when you met her?'

'We missed her,' Miss Pink said.

Lavender, in black with pearls, smiled tightly. 'Have you had a good day?' she asked.

'Quite pleasant, thank you.' Miss Pink was equable.

'But you didn't see Madge.' There was an infinitesimal hesitation before the name as if she didn't like pronouncing it. From behind the bar Hamlyn regarded them both with what might be trepidation.

'We missed her,' Miss Pink said heavily. 'Are you feeling better?'

'I'm fair. I'm afraid I'm always affected by tension. As Kenneth says,' she looked innocently at Hamlyn, 'I shouldn't have come to Skye. There would have been tension anyway—with him climbing every day, but it would have been even worse if I'd stayed at home.'

The colonel said stiffly, 'Non-climbing wives have a great deal to put up with. It's not dangerous really, y'know; much more dangerous crossing the road.'

'I'd feel so much happier if he took a proper guide,' Lavender went on. 'I know Madge Fraser has some certificates but so had that fellow Watkins, and no one could have been more vicious than him. Except a woman. And why has she gone up to the waterfall anyway? I know Vera has suspicions.'

Hamlyn said, 'I really don't think you should express yourself in that vein, ma'am; it might do a great deal of harm if it reached the wrong ears. Press, for instance. Don't you agree, Miss Pink?'

She roused herself from what appeared to have been a stupor.

'Oh, no doubt.' She was vacuous. 'She must have travelled at quite a speed though. On the ridge, I mean.' She beamed at him. 'Have you been out today, colonel?'

In his relief at her turning the conversation, he became verbose. 'I was cutting the grass this morning, and setting traps for those moles, but after lunch I was allowed to go out on the loch for a bit of sport. Hunt was out too. You're having mackerel fillets with fennel tonight.' He looked smug, then anxious. 'You won't be dining on toast, ma'am?' he asked of Lavender.

'Mackerel's so *rich.*'

'The fennel takes care of that.'

'What is to follow?' Miss Pink asked frantically, but then Maynard ran down the stairs and entered the room. He was followed by Betty Lindsay and the conversation remained—innocently and without contrivances—on food.

But Lavender was not to be escaped so easily. After a delicious dinner with venison following the mackerel, Miss Pink was strolling on the colonel's shaven if bumpy lawns when a figure came towards her lit eerily by the Northern Lights.

'One can't stay out,' Miss Pink warned. 'The midges are bad.'

Lavender fell into step beside her. She was smoking and Miss Pink leaned gratefully into the smoke. When she spoke, the other's voice was surprisingly cool and serious.

'What is Kenneth hiding?' she asked.

'Why don't you ask him?'

'I have and he won't tell me. It's something to do with Madge, isn't it?'

'You heard that altercation before breakfast yesterday.'

Lavender ignored this. 'It's something to do with Monday night. And Madge. What does she know?'

Into her voice had crept the familiar ghoulish note. Miss Pink looked round the dark lawns and back at the lighted windows.

'When did your husband leave you on Monday evening?'

'There was a lot of Monday evening. When, between six and midnight?'

'What makes you think he went to Largo?'

In the silence that followed the bats could be heard squeaking, fainter than mice.

'Did Madge say he was at Largo? But how did she know? Ah! *She* was at Largo and saw someone. No—' her tone changed, became firmer, '—that's what she *says*.' The sharp face turned to Miss Pink, the angles accentuated by the wheeling lights. 'You know,' Lavender whispered, 'it could be Madge; she can pull Kenneth up a climb. She's immensely strong.'

Miss Pink took the other's arm as they moved towards the house. Her voice was low. 'You may know too much. As Hamlyn says, it could be dangerous. I lock my door at night. You should as well.'

Lavender stopped abruptly. 'That's ridiculous.' She giggled. 'We're hardly young girls.'

Miss Pink was serious. 'I know it was a sex crime, but no one knows the motive, do they? Besides, that's not the point. You could be dangerous in another way.'

'To her?'

'To someone.'

Chapter 13

THERE WAS A further storm during the night and when morning came the cloud was clamped solid at two thousand feet. The wind was in the south-west and, standing outside the porch after breakfast, Miss Pink remarked to Ken Maynard that it wouldn't be long before the start of the equinoctial gales. When he didn't respond, she turned and saw that he was staring thoughtfully through the trees in the direction of Eas Mor, oblivious of her words and the resulting scrutiny.

His uneasiness was infectious. 'Shall we stroll up the hill and find out how the traverse went?' she asked.

He agreed with alacrity and they put on their boots and went up the drive. Madge owned a white Simca and when she left Glen Shira House she had parked it beside the road at the point where an ill defined path started for the waterfall. They could see the place from the entrance to the grounds but no car was parked there.

'That's quite logical,' Miss Pink said after a moment, and as if they had been arguing, which they hadn't. 'She must have abandoned the traverse at a point nearer Glen Shira than Sliga-chan and descended to the tent direct. She could have retreated down one of the corries farther north and walked down the glen.' Maynard was staring at her and she felt she was gabbling. 'Let's go up,' she said gruffly.

There seemed to be a tacit agreement that hurry would in-dicate anxiety: a feeling that it was possible for them to precipi-tate something; nevertheless, their strides were long and they were breathing hard by the time the tent came in sight. No one was visible, but then they were approaching the back of the tent.

'She's gone to Sligachan to pick up the car,' Maynard said, but his companion was silent as they skirted the guy ropes.

The tent was closed but on the grass at the entrance were the small day sack which Madge used when climbing, strapped and fastened and lying as if it had just been taken off, a pair of boots and navy-blue socks, the latter partly inside out, again as if she'd just pulled them off and left them lying. There were also two or three aluminium billies, obviously forming a set. Everything was soaked by the rain and the frying pan was brimming with water.

'Should we wake her?' Maynard whispered.

Although all the buttons down the front of the tent were unfastened, the flaps were still held together by the small loops at their base slipped over a central tent peg. Miss Pink was eyeing a half-bottle which protruded from under the side of the tent. It held an ounce or two of amber liquid. As she didn't answer immediately Maynard bent and parted the flaps.

'There's no one here!'

'She's gone to Sligachan,' she said, and felt her stomach contract with tension.

'Look!' Lifting the nylon loops off the peg, he threw the flaps wide.

Miss Pink saw a spartan interior: an expanse of ground sheet, a tidily rolled sleeping bag at the back, a big closed rucksack, an old-fashioned biscuit tin and the half-bottle that still contained a little whisky.

They stood back and surveyed the scene.

'She's just come down,' he said, regarding the boots and socks, the day sack which, apart from the rain, still looked as if it had just been swung off its owner's back except that the concavity which the spine makes in an unframed pack had now filled out.

'*Had* just come down,' she corrected.

His look was hostile but impersonal; his thoughts were not on Miss Pink. 'She'd just come down,' he amended, 'very tired;

didn't even trouble to unfasten the tent properly—oh God!'

She had been following her own line of reasoning and his tone shocked her.

'Was someone waiting in the tent?' He was horrified.

'Most unlikely.' She became abstracted again. 'Why the billies? Why start cooking before she'd even opened the tent properly?'

'She didn't trouble; she needed a drink. That whisky bottle's too obvious for anything else.'

'She didn't have any whisky,' Miss Pink said.

'How on earth do *you* know?'

'I don't mean when she came down off the ridge. She didn't have any the day before, when I was up here. She must have bought another half-bottle at Sligachan when she took the car over. She's drunk rather a lot, hasn't she?'

He wasn't listening. He was fitting the billies into their 'nest'. 'This little lid: the pan is missing that it should fit.' Carrying the lid, he walked towards the burn.

'She didn't get water there,' Miss Pink called, herself making upstream to the point where she remembered Madge emerging on Wednesday morning. There was a faint trod which, after about twenty yards, converged with the bank of the burn. At this point some slabby rock intruded into the moor and the way came unpleasantly close to the edge. The drop was about fifteen feet but a few paces further was the place where Madge must have drawn water: a broken rib of rock dropping in easy steps to a sloping slab some twelve inches above the present level of the burn. As she contemplated this she was joined by Maynard.

'What's happened?' he pleaded. 'That gear there—' he jerked his head towards the tent, 'it's been out all night. Where is she?'

Unhappily they started to follow the bank downstream, where, in places, the heather actually overhung the short rock walls. Miss Pink crossed the slabby patch and looked back at it from a vantage point. There was a mossy corner below the slab.

'What's that?' Maynard was standing above the corner, pointing.

'I can't see anything.'

'There's a shoe wedged behind that rock; I'll go down—'

He ran back and scrambled into the burn, stumbling over the boulders to below the corner. She watched and waited with a sense of inevitability. He retrieved the object and stood staring at it, water flowing over his boots, then he waded upstream, climbed the bank and came slowly through the heather. The smell of honey was overpowering. He held out a brown sandal with a flat sole.

'It's hers.'

'How can you be sure?'

He turned away and she didn't press for an answer. They continued down the bank, studying the bed of the stream. After a few yards they saw a light metal pan in the bottom of a pool and, a short distance further, cast like flotsam on a strip of gravel, the second sandal. They didn't retrieve these but continued to the lip of the great fall where they stopped and regarded the water sliding over the edge.

'What do you think?' he asked hopelessly.

'If we can get into the ravine at all, it will be by way of the left bank; the right one is impossible.'

'You think she's—' He gulped air and tried again. 'You think we ought to go down?' He looked at the canopy of birch foliage below them. 'It could be dangerous.'

But she was already crossing the burn to the left bank. He followed and they made their way round the gouge in the moor to a place where the trees stepped down at the least precipitous angle. They descended through a green gloom, slipping and sliding from trunk to trunk, came to a loose bank of shale above the water, crossed the burn, struggled through saplings on the opposite side, then came back again, the sound of the fall increasing until they could no longer communicate except by signs.

They stumbled over rounded boulders to the foot of Eas Mor. Miss Pink was in the lead, concentrating on her footing because the rocks were wet with spray and it had occurred to her that to lie here with a broken ankle waiting for rescue, with the fall thundering above her head, would constitute a peculiar form of horror. She looked up and saw dark globules of water, like tipped rubbish, leap out against the sky. She looked down and saw the body.

The waterfall dropped to a green pool about twenty-five feet wide, and ten feet from the fall the main outlet ran off between two rocks. The body had gone through the rocks and now lay stranded on the slanting shallows beyond.

It was very cold. The fall made air currents like a wind. Miss Pink moved forward, slipping on the stones. There was little doubt that it was the guide; they recognised the breeches and jersey. She lay face-down and barefooted. When they turned her over the features were unrecognisable, but then it had been a long fall.

Maynard walked away and sat down. Miss Pink glanced at his back and then examined the body. The limbs were fractured in many places and quite flaccid. She stood up and, for a moment, had the impression that she was deaf because it appeared that the water was falling without sound. She moved away purposefully and Maynard jumped when she touched his shoulder.

They climbed out of the ravine, the sense of hearing returning as the rush of the fall receded. Now they could distinguish bird calls and the soughing of birches in the breeze. Out on the open moor, Maynard turned to Miss Pink.

'What do we do now?'

'Sit down,' she said comfortably.

'I suppose you're right.' He sat on a heathery ledge and stared at the sea. 'There's no hurry.' Miss Pink said nothing but she was not staring in his hopeless fashion; she was frowning, pondering, and by telepathy, he hit on the subject.

'When did it happen? She'd never slip in the daylight, sober or drunk.'

'There's no stiffness in the body. In normal conditions you'd expect it to be rigid after twelve hours, but then cold delays *rigor*; the night temperature and the water could account for the delay.'

'She must have been worn out. She came straight down from the Banachdich pass to the tent.'

'Worn out after that distance?'

'It's a long way.'

'She'd intended to do the whole ridge.'

'She made a mistake. If she didn't come off because she was tired, why should she come off? What's it matter anyway?'

'Then,' Miss Pink suggested, 'she came off in that brief storm yesterday afternoon or—later?' Her voice rose, puzzled. 'And when she went for water, fell in the burn?' She frowned at him.

'There was the whisky, don't forget that. If it was a full bottle when she started, she accounted for most of it. She must have shrugged off her pack, got out of her boots and just sat there in the heather swigging whisky until she felt like eating. She put her sandals on but didn't trouble to fasten them. That's dangerous. Then she stumbled on that slabby bit and fell down the mossy corner, probably hitting her head. The burn did the rest. I wonder why she drank so much? Of course, it hasn't been her week, and having to retreat from the ridge could have been the last straw on top of all the trouble in the glen.'

This time their thoughts were running on the same lines. He shook his head in a negative gesture. 'No. She'd never do that!'

'Not deliberate?'

'No. Madge lived for her family. She wouldn't have understood suicide, let alone have contemplated the thought for herself.'

'I just wondered.' She sounded meek. 'The burn looks too low to carry a body to the fall. You'd expect it to jam.'

'It rained.'

'It wasn't a spate when we came down.'

'There was another storm in the night.' There was a pause, then he said carefully, 'Why should she kill herself?'

'Terry's killer must have suffered.'

'Not if he's mad.' He was equable. 'Madge wasn't mad.'

'Madness isn't always obvious, but you'd known her for a

147

long time. . . . You'd seen her under pressure—well, on hard climbs. Surely she wasn't always cool?'

'She was worried if things got difficult.' His tone was deliberate. 'And she was relieved afterwards, like anyone else—but this is totally irrelevant. Do *you* think she was a nutter?'

'If she killed herself—'

'She didn't. She had nothing to do with Terry either.'

Miss Pink said: 'Wednesday evening, when you were drinking, you thought Vera turned Madge out of the house because she suspected Madge had something to do with Terry's death.'

'I was drunk. You said so.'

'You've changed your mind?'

He sighed. 'Well, I don't think Madge was having an affair with Hamlyn—why, she only tolerated the old fellow because he was Vera's husband! Perhaps he's having an affair with someone else and lied to Vera about her identity; maybe he was just boasting about Madge.'

'Do they share the same room?'

'Who?'

'Vera and her husband. Do they share a bedroom?'

'Of course they do.' He stared at her as if she'd been overcome by events. 'I'd better go down and report this to the police. And they'll be needing a rescue team to get the body out. Are you coming down?'

'I'll make myself useful looking for an easier way out of the ravine.'

But as soon as he'd disappeared from sight she went back to the tent where she opened Madge's day sack and ran over the contents. The sack was made of waterproof material and the folded anorak inside was quite dry. There was a survival bag, a woollen cap, headlamp, whistle and a tin of Elastoplast, also half a bar of Kendal Mint Cake. There was no other food and no plastic water carrier.

The pass was in cloud, and the gullies which dropped away on the Coruisk side were terrifying. It was not a nice place to be alone, but Miss Pink reminded herself that Madge had often been alone, and she continued searching until, away beyond another jumbled crest, she saw the Stone Man.

It was very quiet; even the wind was soundless, and the mist appeared to move of its own volition. Only the scree shifted noisily under her boots and the sound echoed—or was someone else moving on the scree?

The Stone Man loomed and wavered like a real man above the abyss but she clenched her teeth and went towards it and the thing, as if intimidated, resumed its solidity and waited—smugly? Two bodies had made her fanciful.

The cache was about six feet from its base and, she was almost certain, to the north. She carried no compass for the rocks were magnetic in places and compasses on the Cuillin were unreliable. But the question of degrees was immaterial; the cache was on the Sgurr Banachdich side of the pass and this was it and there was the hole which Madge had said was ideal, and the rock to block the entrance. It was not blocking the entrance any longer and the hole was empty.

She knelt and peered at the scree. There was nothing to show that food had been stored here, or eaten: no shred of paper, not an orange pip nor a crumb of bread, and if the plastic water carrier had ever been in the hole, it had vanished.

Stones moved in a crunching rhythm. This was no echo. Very carefully she rose and moved back from the Coruisk side where the precipices were. The footsteps were coming along the pass from the south. A form resolved itself into a person and suddenly the atmosphere lightened, the cloud drifted away, and Colin Irwin was moving towards her. He looked puzzled rather than surprised at her presence.

'I was on my way to Madge's tent and I met Maynard. He told me what happened. It's ghastly.'

'Why were you going to the tent?'

'I only learned this morning that she'd moved up to the waterfall, and Captain Hunt said that she was doing the ridge yesterday, so I got finished quick and went up to ask her what sort of a trip she'd had.'

'You finished what?'

'The cows and so on. I'm staying at Rahane for a bit. Old MacNeill got a call from Willie yesterday to fetch him home because the police had let him go. I'd been helping out while Willie was at Portree.'

'So Willie was back in the glen last night?'

'No. They never came back: the pair of them.'

'Didn't they phone?'

Irwin grinned. 'Crofters don't publicise their whereabouts.' His face fell. 'But this is awful: Madge falling in the burn! I can't believe it! Can you understand how it happened?'

'She must have been extremely tired to retreat from here—'

'Maynard told me. Why do you think she went down from here? Is the food gone?'

'Every bit of it.' She led him across the scree to the hole near the Stone Man. He looked round him and then up the ridge towards Sgurr Banachdich.

'Who passed you before I came on the scene?'

She blinked at him. 'This morning?'

'Didn't someone go by a few minutes before I arrived? I thought I saw a figure going on towards the summit, but the cloud was shifting about; I could have imagined it—must have done if you say there was no one.' She regarded him fixedly but he didn't notice her expression. He reverted to the tragedy. 'Euphemia said something odd about Madge.'

'Oh yes?'

'She said that she wouldn't camp alone in this glen, if she was paid. She won't stay in Shedog on her own; she sleeps at Sletta with the Hunts. When I pointed out that Madge wasn't afraid of anything, Euphemia said that it would be better if she was, and she said the same thing held with Terry. Isn't that strange?'

'Not really,' Miss Pink said.

He sat on a rock and, after a moment's hesitation, she sat beside him. They looked out from under an umbrella of cloud to the mainland and the Sound of Sleat basking in sunshine. When he spoke again his tone was quiet and conversational and, in view of what he was saying, she realised that he was suffering from shock.

'Funny thing: I always thought it was Watkins who killed Terry, well, not quite true; my initial reaction was that it was Willie: when I found out that he went across to Largo, but I soon realised there had been a misunderstanding. That was after I talked to Willie. He plays the game according to the rules, you see; they're very strict on etiquette, the crofters. But Terry didn't know there were any rules. She didn't give him the ritual brush-off when he went over the first time on Monday evening, so he went back—he told me himself. He thought she was just there for anyone, you see. She'd been Watkins' girl and then she came to me; I expect everyone thought the same thing. He was quite frank about it. But I'm a bit puzzled about Watkins.'

Miss Pink was following this attentively. 'Where does he come in?'

'If it wasn't Willie, the next most likely person is Watkins but is he likely? He knew Terry—and he didn't want her and he was vain. It wouldn't be like him to come across to Largo and risk her rejecting him. Besides, he was drunk.'

'That can be simulated. You're quite sure she would have rejected Watkins—or anyone?'

'We got on. We found out in one day. She said she'd stay on Skye, with me.' He looked at her candidly. 'She meant it. So I can't think she'd invite another guy to Largo in that way. She respected me and it was my place. Do you understand?'

'Yes; she'd found what she was looking for—but did she have all that much regard for her own body? You have to face facts, and she was promiscuous. You're suggesting that she changed suddenly?'

'Am I?' He gave the question thought, gazing down the corrie to the glen where Largo was visible, even at this distance. 'She *wasn't* promiscuous,' he said carefully, 'because that means everybody, and Terry had no time for old or ugly men—'

'Good gracious! What was George Watkins?'

'The exception.'

In the silence that followed, both seemed to be acknowledging the truth of this, then Miss Pink asked, 'Why are you talking about Terry?'

'Well, why not?'

'It is Madge who has just died.'

He stared at her. 'Are you reading some significance into that? Madge died last night, and I talk about Terry who died several days ago? But there was no personal relationship between me and Madge, and I guess her death put me in mind of Terry. Like, you might say: death was the common denominator.'

'You weren't thinking that there was any connection between the two deaths? You see, what you've been suggesting is that Terry's visitor on Monday evening was not a man because she wasn't interested in anyone other than yourself—' he shifted restlessly, '—or, if not that, that she would not have invited a man into your house. That leaves a woman, doesn't it? But the women form a very restricted circle—and one of them has just died. Which is why there could be more than the mere fact of death as a common denominator.'

Chapter 14

ON THE DESCENT they made a wide detour to avoid Eas Mor; neither had any desire to see the body being evacuated. In the context, it was undignified; one would have felt differently had the guide died at work.

Irwin left Miss Pink at the entrance to Glen Shira House and she walked down the drive to find a black police car parked outside the porch, and Lavender Maynard sitting on the seat in front of the Michaelmas daisies.

'The police were asking where you were,' the other said by way of greeting. 'Merrick was annoyed that you'd disappeared.'

'So that is Merrick's car; what is he doing?'

Lavender looked sly. 'Madge was a suspect in the first murder case; naturally the C.I.D. would come back when she was killed.'

'*First* murder case?'

Lavender smiled unpleasantly. 'I mean the first death, of course. This one is an accident, isn't it?'

Miss Pink let that go. 'What is Merrick doing at this moment?'

'He's talking to Kenneth. They got the body down some time ago; they had a lot of difficulty in the ravine. It kept getting tangled in the trees.'

'Were you there?'

'No, but Captain Hunt went up. We've had the Press here and the Mountain Rescue team. Betty and I were helping cut sandwiches in the kitchen. You were lucky to miss all the fuss. You're back early. Where did you go?'

'To Banachdich.'

153

'Why?'

'It's a pleasant scramble.'

'What did Colin Irwin want with you?' Lavender smiled like a ferret. 'He followed you up the corrie. Captain Hunt—'

'—Saw me, and told—Euphemia?'

'And yet,' Lavender said with a startling swing to objectivity, 'although they're so garrulous, they don't give anything away if it's to their disadvantage.'

'And they talk when that is advantageous? Who benefited by publicising my meeting with Colin Irwin?'

'Who indeed? Who stole my sleeping capsules? Two have been taken from a bottle beside my bed.'

'Perhaps you miscounted.'

'I never miscount. Ask Kenneth.'

'Could he have taken them?'

'He won't touch barbiturates; says he can get to sleep by yoga.'

Betty Lindsay came out of the porch wearing an apron, her face red and shining.

'Can I sit here with you? What an awful day! Still, I suppose it's best to keep busy.'

'Is there anything to do?' Lavender asked without enthusiasm.

'No. Euphemia and Ida are coping with the washing up. Vera's gone upstairs for a few minutes' rest.'

Miss Pink said, 'Euphemia is here, despite the police? They drove her away last time.'

'She didn't like the police asking her intimate questions. Of course, they're not doing it this time: taking statements. Only from the last people to see Madge alive. They want you,' she added carelessly. 'They're with Ken at the moment.'

'They'll want Vera,' Lavender said, and smiled.

'I don't see why,' Betty countered. 'This was an accident, not a murder case.'

'Not proved yet,' Miss Pink said. 'It's not official.'

Betty scrutinised her face. 'The Fiscal was up there, and the pathologist.'

'Not at the fall!'

154

'Oh yes. And at the tent.'

'How did the pathologist get here so quickly? Surely they haven't one resident on Skye?'

'He flew up from Glasgow for the autopsy on Terry and was still here when Ken reported the accident.'

'What were the results of the autopsy?'

'I don't know. But I shouldn't think there'll be any surprises. That goes for Madge too—' Miss Pink was regarding her with astonishment, but she went on evenly, 'Ken said she must have drunk nearly half a pint of Scotch. Well, it'll be there in the stomach, won't it?'

'Bloodstream. It's absorbed almost immediately.'

'Like Tuinal,' Lavender put in brightly.

Miss Pink started to say something and checked. 'Why did you say that?' she asked curiously.

'That's what I take: Tuinal.'

'So what?' Betty was brusque.

'Two capsules have been stolen.'

'I expect Madge pinched them. She'd need a good night's sleep before doing the ridge. And after you and Vera had been getting at her, she could have found sleep difficult. She must have taken your capsules: poetic justice.'

'In the circumstances that's a little ironical. I didn't "get at" Madge, not like some people.'

'Just a few choice words at selected moments.' Betty was mildly vicious. 'Although, I must admit, Vera was the one who drove her away. She had good cause though.'

'Had she?' Lavender looked from Betty to Miss Pink. 'I suppose she had.'

'God! She caught the girl seducing Gordon in their sitting room!'

Miss Pink stirred. 'Vera told you that?'

'That's the story that's going around; there was a hell of a row in their sitting room on Tuesday evening. Someone must have heard it and talked.'

'I wonder who?' Miss Pink mused. 'I was the nearest to their sitting room. I heard nothing.' She didn't add that she'd come

155

on the scene too late: as Madge was slamming into the lavatory, presumably just having come—been ejected?—from the sitting room. 'What was Vera's reaction to Madge's death?' she asked.

'It must have been an awful shock,' Betty said.

'She'll blame herself.' Lavender savoured the words. It was obvious that neither of them had been present when Vera heard the news of the tragedy.

From the top of the wood came the clatter of the cattle grid. They watched the drive expectantly and the Hamlyns' Avenger appeared, the back piled high with provisions. The colonel waved to them as he drove round to the stable yard. Betty had leapt up. 'He doesn't *know!* He left just after breakfast! What a shock for him. I must go and give him a hand with that stuff anyway; his back's bad today.'

Miss Pink followed the other with surprising speed. 'What's wrong with his back?'

'Damn! I shouldn't have said that. Don't let on that you know. Vera told me. She didn't want him to drive to Portree; it's agony when he gets these bouts, but he would go. Friday's their shopping day—'

They entered the kitchen to find Ida and Euphemia at the sink. Hamlyn came in the back door with a box full of meat. He greeted the ladies with his usual courtesy but his puzzled glance went to Betty's apron.

'You haven't heard the news?' she asked.

His face went stiff. 'My wife?'

'No. Vera's all right, but Madge has had an accident.'

He didn't relax and pain appeared in his eyes. 'A bad one?'

'I'm afraid so, Gordon.'

He felt for a chair and sat down. The crofting women drew together and watched. 'Dead,' he stated flatly.

After a pause, Betty said: 'I'm sorry.'

He sighed deeply. 'Where did it happen?'

'She fell over Eas Mor.'

He frowned and shook his head. 'What Eas Mor?'

'The waterfall at the back.' She gestured vaguely.

'What? Just over the road—*our* Eas Mor? No.' He stared

at them in disbelief. 'Eas Mor,' he muttered. 'How, for God's sake?'

Maynard put his head round the inner door and beckoned to Miss Pink. Merrick wanted her in the writing room. Leaving Betty to cope with Hamlyn she went out into the passage.

'What kind of mood is he in?' she whispered.

'Not healthy. I'm going up for a bath.' He looked appallingly tired.

A card table had been set up in the writing room and on it was a one-inch map which Merrick and Ivory were studying. They turned at her entrance and she saw that they were tired too. Merrick wasted no time in preliminaries.

'Good afternoon, ma'am; would you show us where you went this morning, and the place where the deceased put this food?'

It was an old map, and the rash of symbols for scree and crags totally obscured the grand design of the Cuillin. She traced the line of her route up Coire na Banachdich to the cache, a proceeding which they observed in silence and, she felt, without comprehension.

They sat at the large table and she gave her statement as it had happened. Ivory took it down in shorthand. Merrick interrupted only on minor points of fact, like the height of the waterfall, but even that didn't constitute a fact. She thought it was about one hundred and twenty feet. Innocently she asked what his estimate was, but he wouldn't commit himself. He glanced at his notebook.

'We have quite a collection of facts,' he said. 'I think I understand some of them, but I haven't got the feel of what happened. I need these facts interpreted by an independent witness who's thinking carefully, not by a rescuer glancing at a big drop and making a guess, and I'm not just talking about the length of the drop. Would you come up to the tent with us and show us how you think it happened? You're not committing yourself; we had to go up there again anyway. You'll be giving expert assistance; neither of us knows anything about mountain country.'

They were wearing gum boots and she felt sorry for them; such footgear must have been perilous in the ravine. As they climbed the slope she was able to indicate the approximate position of the cache, and they surveyed the headwall with some alarm.

'Maynard said a *pass*,' was Ivory's comment.

'It's an easy way to Coruisk and there's no climbing involved.' Seeing their expressions, she added earnestly, 'One can stroll up—and down, at least in daylight.'

Merrick sighed. 'It's another world. No wonder we can't understand it.'

'That back wall of the corrie is innocuous,' she insisted. 'If you saw some of the things that Madge has climbed, you'd say they were impossible. What *I* don't understand is how she fell over a fifteen-foot drop and killed herself.'

It intrigued them. 'That's why we're here,' Merrick said. 'To get that straight. Maynard couldn't help us there: delayed shock, I reckon; she was his guide, wasn't she? When it was obvious you'd disappeared, he suggested you'd gone up to this cache to see if that could tell us anything. Could it?'

'The hole where she put the food is empty.'

'Is it? But are you sure there was food in it?'

'There should have been food and water; I saw her put the water bottle in her pack on Wednesday.'

'Perhaps she never took it up to the ridge.'

'That bottle has to be somewhere. If she didn't take it, it should be in the tent.' He shook his head. 'Then she ought to have brought it down. It wasn't in her small sack; I looked.'

'That's a help to us; your prints are on the headlamp.'

'You compared those quickly.'

'Oddly enough, we had the Glen Shira people's prints in the car when we came over.' They exchanged bland stares. 'What's your feeling about this empty cache, ma'am?'

They were climbing very slowly. Miss Pink, as befitted her sex and years, had the path while the detectives stumbled through the heather.

'One assumes—' she emphasised the verb heavily, 'that she

was tired when she reached the pass—perhaps she'd damaged an ankle—and she decided to come down at that point. She would come straight down the headwall and the corrie to the tent. The objection to that is the absence of food wrappings *anywhere*, either in the hole by the Stone Man or in her pack, and the missing water bottle.'

'I get the impression,' Merrick said, 'that there's a fringe element among climbers who wouldn't be averse to a bit of pilfering. Surely food and drink on a mountain would be most welcome?'

'No one would know it was there. She put a stone across the hole.'

'If it was necessary: this food,' Ivory put in, 'would she have to abandon the trip if it was stolen?'

'It isn't essential, but if she was tired and found there was no food, if she reached the cache during a storm—yes, I think finding it stolen could be the final straw and she'd abandon the trip.'

'Surely that's irrelevant,' Merrick said. 'Whether she ate the food or someone else did, it's most likely she came down the corrie?' After some hesitation Miss Pink nodded, but her expression was doubtful.

They'd come out on the lip of the ravine and now they stopped to look across at the waterfall. She had a sudden vision of a body going over the top and she winced.

'I hope she was dead.'

'If she was alive at the top, death was instantaneous at the bottom.' Merrick had read her correctly.

'I heard that a pathologist came up. Did he help you?'

'Not really, not at this stage. He was surprised to find no *rigor*, but then she was in cold water all night; that would delay it. He'd expect it to set in very quickly once the body was removed from the burn.'

'It was only in a few inches of water; it wasn't submerged.'

'We'll have to wait and see whether she died from a fractured skull or was drowned. You know we have the autopsy on the Cooke girl? Manual strangulation, no pregnancy, no recent intercourse. We're looking for Watkins and Lindsay,' he added grimly. 'None of the common motives for a sex crime apply in Cooke's case—she wasn't pregnant, wasn't raped; perhaps we'll give motive a miss, eh, and just go for the chaps who made off as soon as they saw their chance?' He was angry. Miss Pink asked diffidently: 'Have they left the island?'

'If they have, they didn't take that van. We've got the numbers of all the vehicles going over to the mainland and Watkins' Ford isn't among them.'

They made their way round the lip of the ravine to the top of the fall where Miss Pink followed the bank so meticulously that they were able to inspect every yard of the burn's course.

'We've removed the sandals and the pan,' Merrick told her. She nodded absently. 'What are you interested in now, ma'am?'

'The depth of the water, and the rate of flow.'

'The Fiscal came up here; he said these burns rise and fall very quickly, that there was no question but a body would be carried down when the water was in spate.'

'I agree, but there was no spate yesterday; the burns were very low indeed, and we never had enough rain for a flood.'

The tent was still in position but Madge's possessions had been removed from the grass. Suddenly Merrick said, 'You're a climber, ma'am; could you explain the sequence of events when she came down from the climb: having regard to how her things were disposed when you came up this morning?'

'You mean, a reconstruction?'

'Not physically. If you want, but a commentary on her movements might help. Shall we try it?'

'Yes. Well, she'd approach the tent from the corrie—if one assumes that she came down from the pass—'

'Just a minute,' Merrick interrupted. 'When you came down yesterday with Maynard, can you remember how the tent was?'

'As it is now.'

'With these buttons done up?'

'You couldn't tell from the Coire Lagan path; it's two or three hundred yards away—but the flaps must have been fastened to the peg as they are now or the outline would have looked different.'

'Go on, ma'am; what would be the sequence when she arrives at the tent?'

Miss Pink walked away a few paces, came back and stopped. 'She'd take off her rucksack first—' She glowered at them, trying to identify with the dead guide. 'You've taken the whisky bottle away?'

'Yes.'

She frowned at the tent flaps. 'That whisky would have needed to be remarkably close to the entrance for her to reach inside without undoing the flaps.' She looked at Merrick. 'I think she must have flicked them off the tent peg. She *had* to.'

'She'd take her gloves off first?'

'She wouldn't be wearing gloves.' She smiled politely. 'No one wears gloves at this time of the year; not coming down a corrie anyway.' She flicked back the tent flaps. 'I see you've taken all the gear. She was a tidy person; I think the whisky would have been in the big rucksack that was at the back of the tent, hidden from sight if someone looked in casually. She would have a drink at this point, then she'd take off her boots and socks.'

'The bottle?'

She was puzzled. 'She'd put that down.'

'After screwing the top on,' Ivory pointed out.

She saw that there was more to the whisky bottle than she'd been thinking herself, but she didn't comment.

'After she'd taken off boots and socks, she'd go back to the tent for the billies, disassemble them if they were fitted together, take the little saucepan. . . . At some point she put on her sandals but didn't buckle them. That was unbelievably careless when she was going to climb down into the burn for water. She must have had more whisky. Of course she did! There was so little left. You must take it as read that, between these actions, of finding the billies and putting on her sandals, she takes an odd swig of whisky.'

'Rather a chore, isn't it?' Merrick observed.

161

'I don't follow you.'

'Not so much a chore as a muddle: take a dram, put the top on, fetch the pans, another dram, fetch the sandals, a dram—'

'Maybe she just sat down and drank.'

'Yes, ma'am. You've got your sandals on, unfastened, and you go to the burn with the pan.'

They tramped through the heather to the slabby section above the fifteen-foot wall.

'Maynard showed us where he found the first sandal,' Merrick told her.

'She could have stumbled and gone over here,' Miss Pink suggested, 'or she slipped when she was actually getting the water a few feet upstream, but if there was enough water to carry the body down, you'd expect the sandals to have floated farther.'

'So she went over and hit her head. On what, do you think?'

'Any rock down there.' Miss Pink was morose. 'You can take your pick.'

'The hazards of camping,' Merrick remarked facetiously as they made their way back to the tent. The flaps hung loosely as Miss Pink had left them.

'When are the flaps closed?' she asked. No one answered her. 'Well,' she conceded, 'if there were a sudden shower when she went for water, she could have slipped the loops over the peg to prevent the rain blowing in, but then she forgot to throw her socks inside. Dark, perhaps? And she was drunk.' She looked at Merrick. 'I don't like that whisky. She had none on Wednesday.'

'Maynard told us, so she must have bought another bottle when she took her car to Sligachan.'

'Have you rung Sligachan?'

'No. We will.'

'It's the only explanation,' Miss Pink said, 'that she was drunk. She could never have fallen in a burn sober, not Madge.' Her face creased with bewilderment. 'But you don't drink a great deal of whisky when you come down off the hill; you need pints of fluid like tea. I saw her take a dram once at the end of the day, but another time, when she was thirsty, she drank lager. She'd certainly be dehydrated yesterday; the sun was blazing above the fog.'

'The autopsy will tell us how much she drank, if she drank much.'

'Who would have drunk the rest?'

'If it was a full bottle to start with? That may be difficult to determine. There was one good set of her prints on the bottle, that's all.'

'You'd expect—' She blinked and started as the statement penetrated. '*One* set!' She remembered her reconstruction of Madge's behaviour, the number of times the guide must have handled the bottle. 'It should be covered with her prints!'

'One set,' he repeated, 'and under that it's a mass of greasy smudges.'

'It had been wiped.'

'Or handled by someone with gloves.'

'So that's why you wanted to know if she'd be wearing gloves.' She paused, then stated coldly, 'She had a visitor. That would explain it. He was waiting for her when she came down, he'd got cold and put on gloves. It wasn't cold though. When she arrived he drank most of the whisky; she had one dram and left her prints on it.'

'Then he went down and she fell in the river,' Merrick said baldly. 'The billies have got smudge marks on them too, over her prints.'

'And the pan in the water?'

'Her prints only.'

Back at the house tea was ordered for three in the writing room. Ivory disappeared, and while they waited, Merrick asked Miss Pink who had been absent from the cocktail lounge last evening.

'I was absent myself for a few minutes after dinner; I was in the garden with Lavender Maynard. I didn't notice any gaps before dinner; certainly no one was absent afterwards. Vera Hamlyn joined us. Her husband was behind the bar, and the Maynards and Betty Lindsay were there. Nothing untoward happened at all. I went to bed about eleven. The Maynards had gone up then. I thought the others followed me. You're only interested in the time after dark, surely? Before dark, anyone would have been seen going up to the tent.'

He was thoughtful. 'Unless he'd gone up much earlier, gone in the tent to wait for her, and come down after dark.'

'No one was absent from the house for that length of time.'

Ivory came back and held the door for Euphemia bringing the tea. Her face was blank. When she'd gone, Merrick nodded to his sergeant.

He had telephoned the Sligachan Hotel. One of the maids had been off-duty on Wednesday afternoon when Madge Fraser arrived in her Simca. She'd parked it behind the hotel, locked it, waved to the girl (who knew her by sight), and started straight back. She hitched the first car that came along and it picked her up. She was never nearer the hotel than the lay-by where she left the car, so she didn't buy the whisky there. Her Simca, Ivory added, was still where she'd parked it at Sligachan.

Merrick passed a cup of tea to Miss Pink. 'And you're certain she had no whisky that morning, ma'am?'

'Not certain; I believed her, and I saw the empty bottle.'

'There's no empty bottle among her effects,' Ivory said, handing the scones.

'The Fiscal doesn't like it.' Merrick was gloomy. 'Two violent deaths in four days. Both to young girls. Of course, you *do* get coincidences.' There were long pauses between his sentences. 'The other one was murder. We let Willie MacNeill go yesterday; nothing to hold him on. He was only helping us. Some help he was!'

'Does he still tell the same story?' Miss Pink asked.

'About the woman washing billies in the burn? Funny, both these cases.... Yes, he sticks to that. Why did Madge Fraser leave the house, ma'am? When she asked my permission to do so she intimated that Mrs Maynard objected to her presence here.'

'There was an enormous amount of tension after Terry's death. Everyone was snappy and liable to jump to conclusions.

Vera Hamlyn thought that Madge was too friendly with *her* husband.'

'Anything in it?'

'I—don't know.'

There was a knock at the door and Ida Hunt looked in. 'There's a telephone call for Inspector Merrick,' she told him coldly.

He excused himself and went out. In his absence Miss Pink learned that Ivory disliked hotels and was homesick for his wife's cooking. He wasn't enamoured of the Terry Cooke case; it wasn't what he was used to, except the disposal in Scarf Geo. They were not unfamiliar with bodies on tips; particularly burning tips—

'But drowning will be more familiar,' she put in firmly. 'You'll have had a few of those. Rather run of the mill?'

'Well, no; Madge Fraser is quite interesting: did she fall or was she—' He stopped and grabbed clumsily for a scone.

'The C.I.D. don't investigate accidents.' She was casual.

'We were on a murder case,' he said with dignity, 'and the Fiscal didn't like it.'

Merrick came back. 'Message from the pathologist.' His eyes were keen and hard in the haggard face. 'She was smothered.'

There was a long silence during which Merrick poured himself a second cup of tea, Ivory studied the floor and Miss Pink's mind changed gear. She experienced a blankness at first, then came the awareness that at least some of the pieces were about to click into place.

Ivory spoke first. 'The Fiscal was right then.'

Merrick addressed Miss Pink. 'You expected it, ma'am; you drew our attention to the whisky, and the tent being fastened. Then there was the level of the burn.'

'There was something wrong. But I didn't expect—I'm shocked at the method. What was the rest of the report?'

'It was only a preliminary and only a message. He knew I'd like to know as soon as he discovered that. There's a lot of work to do yet. There are stomach contents and blood to be analysed. But we've got enough to be going on with—' He stopped and regarded her with raised eyebrows. 'And you can vouch for everyone from—when?'

'Six-thirty perhaps; long before dark.'

'Until eleven, except that you say the Maynards went up before. How long before?'

'About a quarter of an hour.'

'Two married couples and Betty Lindsay.' He looked at Ivory. 'We'll see them next, but unless a couple's in collusion, or it's Betty Lindsay, it wasn't done after they went to bed—not, that is, by a resident of this house. Failing that, it was someone from outside, or it wasn't done when we assume it was. We don't know the time of death. Who was the last innocent person to see her alive?'

'So far as we know,' Ivory said, 'the people who picked her up at Sligachan.'

'They'll have to be traced. That still leaves twenty-four hours during which someone must have seen her. We want some help back here.' He was brisk now. He addressed Miss Pink. 'If you'll give Ivory a list of people's movements from when you came down to the house yesterday. . . .' His voice dropped. 'Alibis can be faked—'

'No one can fake his presence,' Miss Pink said stoutly. 'If she was killed when X was under my eye in the lounge, then X can't be the killer, not in this context.'

'That follows. So we have to fix the time of death. What is the earliest time that she could have reached that pass?'

'That's a difficult one. We don't know what time she started, but even if she was north of Alasdair when we reached it, I don't think she'd get to the pass before two, and an hour to reach the tent. . . . But we came down at four-thirty and she wasn't at the tent then! It was closed.'

'Would you see that gear: the little rucksack, the boots and socks, from the path you were on?'

'No, that would be quite impossible.'

'So she could have been there and asleep inside the tent.' He turned to Ivory. 'We'll make a start on people's movements then, double-checking wherever possible. We'll have help within the hour. We'll intensify the search for Watkins and Lindsay because if it was someone outside the house, my money's on them rather than Colin Irwin. And although everyone's under suspicion, it's got to be impressed on them, that no one must do anything, go anywhere, alone. That applies particularly to you, ma'am. Cooke's appears to have been a murder on impulse, but this last one was carefully worked out. There's a very clever killer somewhere and even now, with this second murder, we don't know why he killed.'

Chapter 15

EXCLUDING HERSELF there were thirteen people whose movements the detectives were anxious to determine. Ivory made a list; Miss Pink, searching her memory, told him where people had been to her certain knowledge, but when whereabouts were a matter of assumption or hearsay, the information was queried.

At the end they sat back and regarded each other: Ivory showing resignation, Miss Pink annoyance; there was a query against every name on the list. But as she rejected the possibility of collusion between the married people in the house, she remembered the disappearance of sleeping capsules from the Maynards' room. Ivory noted the information stolidly but lifted his eyebrows at the thought of the killer slipping from the house after dropping Tuinal in a nightcap.

As for the movements of the crofting women: Ida had waited at dinner and subsequently there had been glimpses of her and Euphemia, and Vera Hamlyn, in the kitchen, when Hamlyn went through for ice. The women had gone home about eight thirty. After that they were an unknown quantity as, indeed, were Captain Hunt and Irwin for the whole of the period under review: yesterday afternoon and evening—and night.

Lindsay, Watkins and the two MacNeills were the remaining suspects, and the only help she could give there related to the MacNeills. She repeated Irwin's information that the old man had gone to Portree, ostensibly to join Willie. The son had left the police station at eleven o'clock yesterday morning, Ivory told her. The MacNeills seemed to have vanished between Portree and Glen Shira.

168

At five-thirty Euphemia served Miss Pink with a large sherry and she went upstairs to steep gently in her bath. Before she dressed, she made a personal list. She wrote: 'Where is the water bottle, and why is it missing?'—'Why was the tent fastened?'—but almost immediately she answered that one: 'To delay discovery.' She contemplated this at length, then queried it. The third question needed careful framing: 'If X took the whisky to the tent in order to get Madge drunk, how was she induced to drink it?' and 'Is half a pint sufficient to stop the victim struggling when smothered?' No one could imagine Madge being easy to kill.

Despite the proliferation of queries she felt that this piece of paper was more apposite than the one which Ivory had prepared, although the latter was also based on her information.

She dressed and went down to the kitchen where she found Euphemia blanching sorrel.

'Where is Mrs Hamlyn?'

'She's at the boat, miss.'

'Is she going fishing?'

Euphemia strained the sorrel through a sieve. 'She might.'

'How did she take the news of Madge's death?'

There was a flicker in Euphemia's eyes. 'She—didna like it.'

'She must be very worried.'

'We all are.' The woman turned her back and, lifting the lid of a fricandeau pan, interested herself in the contents, pushing steak around with a fork and mumbling.

'Where is the colonel?'

'He went upstairs a while back.' Euphemia turned quickly and through the window they saw Vera Hamlyn cross the yard to the stables carrying a petrol can.

Miss Pink went out of the back door. In the stable Vera was wiping her hands on a piece of rag. She gasped as the other's shadow fell across the doorway.

'Sorry to startle you,' Miss Pink apologised. 'Going for a trip?'

'Just filling her up.' There was a pause. 'Are they keeping an eye on me?'

'Should they?'

'They should watch everybody until the killer's found.' She seemed quite composed. 'What are they doing now?'

'They're checking on people's movements last evening. When did you know that Madge was murdered?'

'Actually, the inspector started with Gordon: wanting to know where everyone *else* was, of course.' She was coolly amused. They were still standing inside the stable, looking across the yard to the kitchen where Euphemia had been joined by Ida.

'I've got no regrets,' Vera said.

After a moment, Miss Pink asked, in the same companionable tone, 'Not even about her child?'

'Yes, I have there; but the grandmother is comparatively young. Madge would have made a bad mother; it's better this way. She was unstable. All that cold dedicated manner, and the ruthless-mother bit: it wasn't an act, but it was only one side of her. The other side was ruthless too; she was totally amoral. When Madge wanted a man, she took him without any thought at all for the consequences.' Vera gave Miss Pink a quiet smile. 'And no fear. That was her mistake. Madge was the classic victim. I'm only amazed it didn't happen before; her child's father was a married man, too.'

'When did you go up there?'

'Up where, dear?'

'To the tent.'

'My prints weren't found there.'

'What did you do with the water bottle?'

Vera's face was a mask. 'Water bottle?'

'What's wrong with your husband's back?'

'A slipped disc.'

'Is he having treatment?'

'No one knows he has a damaged spine, except me—and you. Presumably Betty Lindsay told you. I'm getting careless.'

'I wouldn't say that.' The tone was dry. 'What was the point of washing the billies at Largo?'

The leap to a different murder was followed without effort. 'I assume: to confuse the issue?'

'And who was the man in the burn?'

'What man, dear? Washing the dishes? Willie only heard mumbling; he didn't hear a woman and a man, but a high and a low mumbling: easy enough to imitate the low register.'

'Terry was dead at that moment?'

'Was she?'

'A curious thing,' Miss Pink said, 'I would have thought the only woman in this community strong enough to carry a body was Betty Lindsay.'

'Poor Betty; what a lot she's had to take.' Vera spread her fingers and studied the back of her hand. 'I have to do all the heavy work round here because of Gordon's back, and then I was in the Land Army during the war.' She smiled. 'No self-starters on tractors in those days, and no discrimination in favour of women. Sacks of corn weighed two hundredweight.'

'How did you meet your husband?'

'During the war.'

'What is his background?'

Vera raised delicate eyebrows. 'Just normal, dear; his father was a rector, nothing interesting.' Nor, her tone implied, that concerned Miss Pink. 'I must see to the dinner,' she went on, then hesitated. 'Mustn't I?'

'Yes.' Miss Pink was grave. 'Where is your husband?'

Vera stood still and eyed her carefully. 'You mean, what has happened to him, don't you? He was in our sitting room.'

Miss Pink followed her indoors, went upstairs, along the passage and pushed open the door of the Hamlyns' sitting room. It was empty.

She went downstairs again and looked in the cocktail lounge. Maynard was behind the bar serving his wife and Betty Lindsay.

'Where is the colonel?'

None of them knew and no one commented on the question. Maynard asked if she would take a sherry but she said not at that moment.

Down the hall a door opened and, looking out, she caught a glimpse of Ida going back to the kitchen. She went and knocked at the door of the writing room. Ivory opened it and Merrick said cheerfully, 'Come in; have you got something for us?'

'Vera Hamlyn has just implied that she killed Madge, and Terry as well.'

'It's a common occurrence in murder cases, ma'am, particularly where there's ladies of a certain age. We've got a lot of those here; I'm not surprised that one of them should confess. Have you anything else?'

'The colonel's disappeared.'

'Oh, I doubt it. He's probably gone fishing. He was with me till six and then said he might go out for a while on the loch. He's not looking at all well; damaged his back earlier this year when he was picking up a stretcher.'

'Could he help you on people's movements?'

'He confirms your statement that all the residents were in the bar last evening until eleven. He was last up: about a quarter past. The house was locked but the back door key's on a nail in the passage. Betty Lindsay says she was in bed at eleven. No alibi, of course. No one could have gone up to the tent in the afternoon according to Hamlyn; he was around all day and has a fair idea of everyone's movements—including your own, incidentally. So far as the people here are concerned, Ida Hunt's recollection agrees with his. As for the crofters themselves, after eight-thirty Euphemia was at Sletta with the Hunts and she slept there. The crofters are scared. We haven't got to Irwin yet. We've discovered what happened to the MacNeills though. Hamlyn ran across them at lunch time today in one of the bars in Portree, so Ivory asked our people if the MacNeills had been seen last night. They had toured every bar in Portree and ended with Willie being forcibly ejected!'

'Who could eject Willie?'

'He was very drunk. His father was no better but more amenable. The MacNeills can't be in the running for this murder. Now, have you got anything else for us, ma'am?'

A telephone was ringing as she returned to the cocktail lounge.

'I'll have that sherry now, Ken.'

'Had a bad time, dear?'

'Not really.' She frowned at him. 'Why "dear"?'

'Just a mannerism.'

'What?'

'You're not with it. Have they shaken you?' He glanced at the other women. 'We're all friends here.'

Someone came quickly and heavily along the hall. A door slammed. They were silent, straining their ears.

'Are there many police in the glen?' Miss Pink asked, trying to make conversation. It would seem too contrived to talk about anything else.

'There are several fresh cars on the camp site,' Betty told her, 'and Ivory said they can bring in a mobile murder control centre to make the investigation on the spot much more efficient. I want to get away. I'm going to look for a croft tomorrow if Merrick will let me go.'

'Couldn't we climb?' Maynard asked wistfully. 'The police won't let us leave the glen but they might let us go on the ridge.' Lavender didn't look at him. She was smoking thoughtfully.

'Miss Pink!'

They all jumped. She looked across the hall and saw Merrick beckoning. Ivory was hurrying away. Merrick looked excited. He drew her into the writing room and closed the door.

'Is Mrs Lindsay in the lounge?'

'Yes.'

'Her husband and Watkins are at Coruisk. Will you show me?'

'It's on the other side of the Cuillin.' She indicated the loch on the map.

'That's only five miles away!'

'Well—'

'There's this climbers' hut. Where is it?'

'Where the outlet from the loch runs into the sea.' She showed him. 'How do you know they're there?'

'An Elgol man took them round yesterday in his boat. Apparently Elgol is the place where you get a boat for Coruisk? It's them all right; they left Watkins' van at the boatman's croft. How long would it take to walk to Eas Mor from this hut?'

'By the quickest way—' She looked at the map and calculated, 'Something like three to four hours over the Banachdich pass.'

He nodded. 'Time enough to do it. Will you tell Mrs Lindsay her husband has been located, and where, and watch her reactions? I'm going round to Elgol by road now but I'm leaving a car at the head of the glen to make sure no one leaves until I give the word. I'll send some people back to carry on the work here, and to give you moral support in case ...'

'In case it's not Watkins or Lindsay?'

He pursed his lips. 'Just keep them together tonight, that's all I ask.'

Betty was neither surprised nor alarmed at the news. From their lack of reaction it was evident that none of the people in the cocktail lounge thought that Andrew Lindsay, nor even George Watkins, was a murderer.

Vera opened the door at the back of the bar to tell them that dinner was ready. She accepted a gin from Maynard and remained with them to drink it, smiling a little nervously, which was not like Vera. When Miss Pink caught her eye, she didn't look away or blink, but her face was suddenly expressionless.

They went in to dinner, drew the tables together and re-laid the places. Ida entered and regarded the new arrangement without comment or surprise. Maynard ordered a Burgundy.

'Where's Gordon?' Betty asked, fiddling with her glass. People murmured negatively.

'You're very quiet, dear.' Maynard addressed his wife. 'You've hardly said a word all evening.' She looked at him without subterfuge, then at Miss Pink who said: 'If you know something, you should tell us. It's dangerous to hang on to knowledge.'

Maynard gave her a quick glance. 'Is that what Madge did?'

Lavender bit her lip and said to Miss Pink, 'It was someone she saw in the wood, wasn't it?'

Ida came in with the steaks.

174

'No starters,' Maynard murmured. 'So what?'

'You can have as much steak as you like,' Ida said tightly. 'There's enough and to spare.'

She went away and returned with the Burgundy, which was cold. Having filled their glasses, she retreated to the sideboard where she hovered like an uneasy ghost. They did not revert to the murder. The incongruities in the normally superlative service intimidated them as much as Ida's unwonted presence. Maynard, as if in defiance of an atmosphere which teetered on the edge of an abyss, ordered a second bottle of Romanée-Conti.

So they were quite a while over their dinner but Ida, far from being resentful, seemed grateful for their company. When they returned to the cocktail lounge the two crofting women lingered after they'd served coffee and liqueurs.

'Where is Mrs Hamlyn?' Miss Pink asked, knowing it was a ritual question requiring a ritual answer—which was duly supplied by Euphemia: 'Gone to their sitting room to rest.'

Miss Pink started to pour coffee. Ida, who had brought in the tray, lifted the flap of the counter, went behind the bar and stood mutely beside Euphemia. The door to the kitchen was closed. Miss Pink paused, took a banknote from her bag and handed it to Maynard.

'Ask the women to take a dram with me.'

The coffee was handed silently.

'Draw the curtains, Betty.' She was wary of the dusk outside.

The telephone rang. Ida and Euphemia looked at each other.

'Mr Maynard will go with one of you,' Miss Pink said comfortably.

When they'd gone, Lavender murmured, 'She was never jealous; I knew that. As if I wouldn't know! She was just playing the part.'

'If she wasn't jealous,' Miss Pink said, 'what was her motive?'

'She was mad. Did you see her eyes tonight? She killed Terry, Madge found out, so she had to be killed too. Gordon must know as well, because she could only have gone up to the tent after we'd gone to bed, and they share a room.'

Maynard and Ida came back. Maynard said, 'It's a professor;

that would be the pathologist, wouldn't it? He wants Merrick. Says he'll speak to you.'

The voice at the other end of the line was pleasant and cultured. The professor (who climbed) knew about Miss Pink and was prepared to chat. At length he reverted to the purpose of his call and, hearing that Merrick was on his way to Coruisk, said he would leave his message with the police station but meanwhile would she relay the salient points should the inspector return direct to Glen Shira?

A moderate amount of alcohol had been found in the bloodstream, he continued conversationally, and it was a moment before she realised he was speaking of Madge Fraser—along with a significant quantity of a barbiturate. The specific figures were in his report.

'A barbiturate,' she repeated stupidly.

'Sleeping pills.'

She said nothing.

'Are you there?' he asked with a twinge of petulance. 'The whisky in the bottle was unadulterated. Yes, and another interesting point is the time of death. Merrick was eager to tie that down, wasn't he? I believe you remarked on the flaccidity of the corpse. Not remarkable if she was killed late last night and the body in cold water throughout, but you'd expect rigidity to set in quickly. It's now—what?—eight hours since she was taken out of the burn, but there's no stiffening. In other words, *rigor* has come and gone; she's been dead well over thirty-six hours. Makes a difference, doesn't it?'

'Yes, it makes a difference.'

She promised to pass on the message, put down the receiver and turned away to find Maynard and Ida regarding her with a kind of apathy and realised that this was their defence mechanism against a new shock. She led the way back to the cocktail lounge and told them. There were no police here as yet and she felt that these people had a right to know everything.

Maynard's apathy evaporated and his face was keen and intelligent again. Betty, for the moment, was vacuous.

'What does it mean?'

'My sleeping capsules,' Lavender said.

Maynard was staring at Miss Pink. 'Dead over thirty-six hours? But that means she couldn't have done the ridge! All the time we were waiting for her on Alasdair.... In fact, she must have been killed Wednesday night and when we went up Thursday morning she was lying at the foot of the waterfall. Her boots and pack were probably outside the tent at that moment just as she'd put them down when— Oh no, *she* didn't put them there; the killer did, and threw her sandals and the saucepan in the burn ... on Wednesday night.'

'Who was absent?' Lavender asked. 'I was in our room; I wasn't well.'

'Apart from yourself,' Betty said, unaware of the *faux pas*, 'no one could have gone up; we were all here—except—' She clapped a hand to her mouth.

'Come off it!' Maynard chided. 'Andrew hadn't the ghost of a motive.'

'He wouldn't have stayed on the island,' she said wildly. 'He wouldn't have gone to Coruisk.' She checked herself. 'The police are watching the ferries,' she added tonelessly. 'That's why they stayed; they couldn't get away.'

Maynard had paid no attention. 'The cache was robbed!' he exclaimed.

'Emptied by the killer,' Miss Pink agreed, 'to add colour to the presumption that she had done the ridge. It explains the absence of the water bottle. It couldn't be put in her day sack because the scene at the tent had already been set and the tent couldn't be visited again. The tent was closed for the same reason that the cache was rifled: to delay discovery and falsify the time of death, all designed to suggest she had been on the ridge and so couldn't have been killed before Thursday evening. The implication was that an accident occurred not long after she came down off the ridge.'

'Someone had a perfect alibi for Thursday,' Maynard breathed.

'And none for Wednesday.'

'When was it done?' he mused. 'No one—' he glanced at

Betty apologetically, 'but no one who matters, was absent Wednesday evening; it must have been done at night, like rifling the cache. No one's been away for long enough to get up to the ridge in the daytime—surely?'

'Night time would mean collusion,' Miss Pink pointed out. 'I mean, if it was someone from the house.'

'I don't see why.' Betty was bewildered.

The door behind the bar opened slowly and Captain Hunt stood there, surveying the company. 'They's all here,' he said over his shoulder. He moved forward, followed by Colin Irwin whose pale hair was restrained tonight by the red brow band. At Miss Pink's invitation they came quietly into the lounge. The captain carried a shot gun.

'That's us all here,' he repeated with satisfaction. 'There's lights coming down the glen. That'll be the poliss.' He looked at his wife. 'Are they after taking guns?'

'I havena looked.'

He went out with Irwin. In the ensuing silence they heard the faint clatter of the cattle grid.

'The colonel's alive then?' Lavender said loudly and everyone stirred and looked at her reluctantly but no one spoke.

The men returned carrying a rifle and another shot gun. Captain Hunt looked at Miss Pink. 'She's taken her own rifle.'

Someone gasped. There was a noise of wheels on gravel, doors slammed, and large men started to fill the hall, some in uniform.

'Come in,' Miss Pink said yet again. 'You have an easy job—in one way. Everyone is here—except the owners.'

'And where are they, miss?' asked a man with an air of authority. Miss Pink looked towards Captain Hunt.

'I heard the engine of the colonel's boat,' he said, 'just before I came up.'

'Which way did the boat go?'

'There's only one way; it put to sea, of course, but there was no way of telling who was in it, nor how many.'

178

Chapter 16

THE POLICE HAD come to guard the people in the settlement—and to make sure they stayed there. Since everyone except the Hamlyns was gathered under one roof, they had nothing to do but wait for daylight and Merrick's return. So they waited: behind closed windows and drawn curtains, in a fug of smoke and a background noise of coffee cups and snores and snatches of conversation. But upstairs, Miss Pink's room was quiet and fresh, her window open towards the sea, and it was not surprising that, at some time during the night, in a state between sleeping and waking, she should have been the only person to hear a shot.

She got up and went to the window. The night was dark and still. She stood there for some time listening to faint animal sounds in the darkness: something that might have been a rabbit's scream, and leaves rustling in the wood under quiet paws. Then she heard the second shot, and it seemed to come from the southern headland.

It was four o'clock. She dressed, without haste, in her climbing clothes, made a pot of tea and filled a flask, then left the house by way of the fire escape—which was unguarded. Someone would have been round in the night to make sure its door was locked but that was only to prevent entry. There was no one and nothing to stop her getting out.

The path to the headland was rocky and she wouldn't use her torch so she had to go slowly, particularly when she crossed the burns which cut back deeply into the moor. The tide was making and the loch calm, the only sounds the splash of a larger wave, or water dripping off some unseen platform. Now and again, by small cliffs (they were low on this side), and from some submerged hole would come faint thuds and a long, heaving sigh.

This peninsula lay south-west of the Cuillin and was bounded on the east by the peak of Gars Bheinn which dropped steeply to the sea. As she approached the headland, the mountain was silhouetted against the dawn and, close at hand, the lochan by the Boat Port gleamed like an opal in the black moor.

The Boat Port had been used as shelter for over two thousand years. There was a ruined village inland and a crumbling fort on the cliff. Someone was standing by the fort and out in the loch a little boat rocked on the water. No one was in it.

Miss Pink paused. 'Have you shot him?'

Vera shook her head. In that grey light she looked so old that, but for the rifle, she might have been one of the people from the ruins.

'Is he dead?'

'Yes, he's dead.'

Miss Pink took off her rucksack at that and produced the thermos flask. Kneeling on the grass she poured tea and looked up, holding the cup.

'You'll be needing this. You can put the rifle down; I know you didn't kill the girls.' When the other made no move, she went on, 'There are no witnesses to what we say. In any case, I know that you won't shoot me. Here, take your tea.'

Vera stepped to the fort and leaned the rifle against the stones, then came and sat down. They ignored the empty boat and looked westward towards the Long Island. The cloud cap over Rum glowed with refracted colour. Behind them, the Cuillin corries held the darkness while the crests were gilded against an expectant sky.

'I never convinced you then?'

'Not really.' Miss Pink accepted the cup and drank her share with appreciation. 'It's been a matter of character,' she said, 'or—more correctly—of people behaving out of character. You called me "dear" when you were stalling, when you were not sure how much of the truth to tell; because some of it was true, and some was partly true. Obviously, you had a strong reason for driving Madge away, but jealousy was inappropriate—for you. And seduction was out of character for Madge. All the same, I was convinced that you were sincere in trying to get rid of her—'

'Oh, I was sincere, I was desperate! Both times—but with Madge more than Terry. I wanted Terry to go for her own protection, but Madge was my friend. She'd still be alive if I'd warned her.'

Miss Pink said, 'I can see why Madge had to be killed but what was the motive for Terry, I mean, specifically? Or was it that she embodied what he was most afraid of: lack of control, animal high spirits—?'

'Look,' Vera was suddenly impatient, 'tell me what you're talking about.'

Miss Pink was startled, then she understood. 'You're conditioned to fighting for him. It's time to relax now. That wasn't a trap to make you start talking. I'll tell you what I think happened.

'Terry was sun-bathing all day: half-naked, naked, it doesn't matter. I suspect he gave himself different reasons for going across to Largo, all highly moral and all invalidated because he went over after dark.' Vera made a protesting gesture. 'It had to be after dark,' Miss Pink insisted, 'because he would never have killed her and left the light on. I saw it at eight-thirty. It went out about ten-thirty; that's when she was killed.'

'Someone else could have—'

'He needn't have had homicidal motives when he went across,' Miss Pink went on firmly. 'Not conscious ones, anyway.... He went across when no one was in the bar. I don't know what he said to her; perhaps he was bluff and jolly for a moment but Terry would go through that like a knife through soft butter. He would bluster and she'd laugh at him; and ridicule was—literally —fatal for her, although it's possible he strangled her just because she raised her voice. Then he panicked—although he remembered to put out the light. He came blundering back through the wood and went straight up the back stairs to your sitting room and told you.'

Vera sighed heavily but said nothing.

'So your confession about washing the billies was correct,' Miss Pink went on. 'And you had to imitate a man to get rid of Willie MacNeill. If he'd continued to think that you were Terry and that she was on her own, he'd have come down in the burn to join you. Washing the billies widened the period in which she could have been killed and lengthened the list of suspects. Her body might never have been found. Putting it down Scarf Geo would be your idea, and it was you who told him to use his own pack frame and a plastic bag from the Rescue Post, and by that time you'd got him to wear gloves, although of course, you'd have seen to it that he put his prints all over the frame again when he'd disposed of the body. It wouldn't have done to have the frame covered with glove smudges. You wore gloves too, when you wiped his prints at Largo, rubber kitchen gloves?'

'Fine plastic,' Vera said, 'like surgical gloves. So I never convinced you about his bad back either? I didn't like that; it came too late, didn't it?'

'Not only that, but you insisted too much on your own strength. At twenty perhaps, not at fifty. You haven't the muscle to carry a body for a mile, and how would you ever lift it over the fence at the end?' Miss Pink regarded the other with compassion. 'And then there was the style of the murders: the differences and the similarity. Terry's was a murder on impulse, Madge's was carefully planned. There *was* a plan in Terry's case but it came after death: the disposal of the body.' Miss Pink looked across the water to Scarf Geo. 'It was quick, simple and, even if it didn't succeed completely, partial success was sufficient for your motives. That particular job,' she added thoughtfully, 'with your collusion, was done in the middle of the night. Nothing else was.' Vera started and stared at her. 'Because there was no collusion on the others,' Miss Pink pointed out. 'On the other hand, Madge's murder was so involved: the drugging in advance—and no barbiturate in the bottle—'

'How did you know that?'

'The *post mortem* result. He must have taken a cup with him; he didn't empty the capsules into the bottle. He was too clever: trying to reproduce the first murder, at least by falsifying the time of death. Vanity? Either he lost sight of the fact that yours was the brain behind the first, at least in the disposal and cleaning up—' Vera winced, '—or he remembered your contribution—he could hardly forget it, and thought he could emulate it.

'I thought that in some form Terry's was a sex murder—but Madge's wasn't. And although it wasn't until late in the day that we knew Madge's *was* murder, there had been a mystery earlier: two mysteries. Why did you quarrel with her, and who did she see in the wood the night Terry was killed? She saw someone because when I told her that Willie's evidence implied Terry was alive at eleven, she became hysterical with relief. So who did she see? Maynard? But she hinted it was him so I argued that it couldn't have been. He was a stalking horse for someone else. You? If it had been you, your quarrel with her wouldn't have been in public on Wednesday morning. That quarrel had a staged quality, like the rumour you spread about her supposed affair with your husband. Both covered the real reason that she had to go.'

'And I didn't succeed,' Vera said tiredly. 'I thought she'd leave the island and she went to Eas Mor: a sitting duck.'

'That was not your fault.' Miss Pink was at her most sincere. She went on, 'Madge was protecting someone, and you were the only person with whom she had an emotional relationship. Otherwise, as you maintained yesterday, a very cool customer, but not interested in men. She certainly wasn't after your husband, but if he were the person she saw in the wood, she might protect him for your sake.

'And then there was the attitude of the crofters towards you. At first I thought they were protecting Willie but they showed more than casualness when he was taken into custody, they appeared relieved, so it wasn't him. It seemed to me that the only incomer for whom they had respect—apart from Irwin whom they seemed to look on as one of themselves—was you. And yet there was an absence of that kind of paternalism which one gets with protection: a kind of jealous regard for the person protected. It wasn't till last night that I realised what the crofters were doing; they were leaving you an open field. It wasn't their business, and they saw to it that other people should be kept in ignorance because it wasn't their business either. Old MacNeill's nerve seems to have broken, probably because Willie was too vulnerable in Glen Shira. Since he was at Largo at a critical time, the killer might think he knew more than he was telling —so as soon as Willie left the safety of the police station, old MacNeill picked him up and kept him in Portree.'

Vera said, 'I got Euphemia to tell old MacNeill to stay away from the glen with Willie, until I said they could come back. I was afraid he would kill Willie next—or Lavender.'

'Lavender?'

'She knew I wasn't jealous. She knew there was something more important, and Lavender is inquisitive. I hadn't much influence left with him. After Tuesday night he thought of me as being on Madge's side, at least while she was alive.'

'It was Tuesday that Madge told him that she'd seen him in the wood?'

'Yes. The police had arrived and were with you in the writing room. Gordon brought you tea and Merrick kept him there, do you remember? At that time Madge was upstairs with me in our sitting room. I thought she was subdued and I'd been trying to draw her out as to what was bothering her. You realise that until then she hadn't attached any importance to hearing Gordon blundering through the wood the evening before; if she guessed he'd come from Largo, she'd have thought he'd merely had a tiff with the girl. All day Tuesday she was on the other end of the Cuillin and she heard that Terry had been killed only when she got back, with Maynard. That's why she was preoccupied in our sitting room.

'When Gordon came up from talking to the police, I left them for a few moments and I went down to make some coffee. I was away too long.'

'Did he attack her? She accused him?'

'She didn't accuse him. She asked him what story he had given the police.' She turned to Miss Pink angrily. 'That girl was ready to work out a story to dovetail with his, to cover him, just because she and I were friends!'

Miss Pink nodded in agreement. 'A very loyal person. The relationship between you was alive and active; Terry was dead, and your husband was merely a pawn. If Madge had had any respect for him she wouldn't have died, because she'd have known it was too dangerous to stay in the glen.'

Gratitude filled Vera's face, then it hardened. 'I don't know how he reacted when she asked him what his story for the police had been. He would have blustered; she would have become impatient—not realising that I knew everything, and wanting to get her questions answered before I came back. He told me, as if in justification of his attacking her, that she was "without a trace of feeling"—for Terry, he meant! He denied everything, so she told him she'd seen him in the wood. I came in just after he'd thrown himself on her. She was in an easy chair and his weight held her down. I rushed over and hit him across the bridge of the nose. Of course, I had no idea what had led up to that but I pretended to misunderstand. It seemed to strengthen his position if I was ignorant of what had happened at Largo.'

'Or it could have been that your mind refused to accept that here was another homicidal attack.'

'Possibly. At any rate, after I'd bawled her out for seducing my husband—I'll never forget the way she looked at me, she was in pain too; he'd got her by the throat—she left, and then he told me about her seeing him in the wood. I thought at first that I'd go to her room and work out a story; after all, she'd been prepared to do that originally, but I held back—for her sake. I felt it was too much to ask after what he'd done to her. Do you know, I don't think she realised that he'd tried to kill her? Or did she think he was always violent towards women? Otherwise why did she accept the whisky the following night?'

'She was a strange person,' Miss Pink said, 'like Terry. It was as if the powers of assessment were concentrated in one direction;

in Madge's case: towards rock, and that all normal sense of caution regarding human beings was lacking. One wonders if judgement had never developed, or had got partway and atrophied. I can understand Madge stubbornly refusing to be driven away until she'd done the traverse of the ridge, but her moving to Eas Mor was an open invitation to the killer.'

'It was suicidal! She should have gone to Sligachan. I wanted to warn her, but would I have been able to make her go even if I told her the truth? I compromised and watched Gordon. He stayed down all Wednesday; he knew I was watching—and then he came to me and told me he couldn't bear to see me so anxious about Madge's talking; that she never would, she thought too highly of us. In a roundabout way he told me that she had nothing to fear from him and I could stop worrying ... but if he'd said he was going on the hill on Thursday, I'd have gone with him. I was completely hoodwinked at the times when he did go up there.'

'In the fog on Wednesday,' Miss Pink put in, 'while we were at dinner and you were serving in the kitchen, and again, while you relieved him in the bar and we thought he was in the Rescue Post.'

'He told me this evening—last evening.' Vera was listless. 'She accepted the whisky. She wasn't in the least frightened. He told me that her not being afraid made him angry. I can see a mad logic in Gordon's actions.'

'Oh yes.' Miss Pink was definite. 'He was able to justify himself: on the premise that he was a superior person.'

'He said to me, "She ought to have been afraid! It was unnatural!" He asked her to forgive him, said I'd sent him up. He wished her well on the traverse and said that we both expected her to come back to the house when "it had all blown over".'

'He told you all that?'

'Yes. He said she was quite friendly. My guess, knowing Madge, is that even in those circumstances, she was a little bored—'

Miss Pink nodded. 'She would be.'

'And then he produced the whisky and a wee metal cup he carries and they drank to her climb the next day.'

'My God!'

Vera's voice was cold. 'And he came away, and went back when she was comatose and smothered her with a jersey in a plastic bag. He was clever enough to know the jersey on its own would leave fibres.... He put the rucksack outside the tent, the billies—you know all the rest. Except before, before—' She shuddered uncontrollably.

'She was dead when he threw the body over,' Miss Pink said gently.

Vera smiled—a kind of smile. 'How long does it take to die with a jersey and a plastic bag over your face?' It was Miss Pink's turn to shudder and then she noticed that Vera was staring fixedly at the water, but the only sign of life was a pair of gannets patrolling lazily. 'Drowning takes four minutes,' she said.

'And the cache?' Miss Pink asked on a high note. 'He emptied that yesterday, on his way to Portree.'

'He left the car in the forest, along the forestry road, and went very fast up Coire a' Ghreadaidh.'

Miss Pink nodded. 'Both Irwin and I heard him in the mist; Irwin thought he saw him—he did see him. Hamlyn left the Stone Man just before I got there. He must have heard me coming. He was cutting things very fine. The water bottle and the food would have been thrown down some gully....'

'He was over the edge,' Vera said. 'Mad. It would have taken only a minor thing to make him kill again. Either that or suicide. He was obsessed by death and seemed to have got other people's muddled with his own, as if killing them was a form of suicide?'

Miss Pink accepted it as a question. 'It *was* suicide before the end of capital punishment, and with mad people there will still be that tradition: murder, then suicide. How did it all start? Because his background is at the root of this—' she gestured towards the water, 'and it was a question about his roots which put an end to our conversation yesterday evening. I don't think he was raised in a rectory.'

'It was a Barnardo's home, but it wouldn't have started there.

Where does anything start? What made his mother abandon him? Why did his father—? That's stupid. Why does any man sleep with a woman?'

'You can go back to the Garden of Eden,' Miss Pink conceded, 'but it's not necessary. I take it he was illegitimate and abandoned and brought up by Dr Barnardo's people. How well he did for himself. Up to a point,' she added.

'Things might have turned out all right if he'd been an ordinary boy,' Vera said, 'but he was above average intelligence. I don't know whether the drive for success was a matter of genes or of conditioning; something of both, wouldn't you say?'

Her companion nodded. 'Often success stops at the end of a stage but obviously he transferred to a similar environment and found another ladder?'

'He joined the Army as a boy recruit, and he was commissioned at the outbreak of the war. He was a good officer: cool and brave and a strong disciplinarian. That was his guiding principle. He could assert discipline, and accept it. He knew his place.' She paused and watched a gannet fall like a stone against the far headland. A spurt of water rose behind it. 'He had rages,' Vera went on, 'but he had iron control. I think I was the only person who saw him lose his temper. A spaniel was wished on us once when some friends were posted suddenly. It was spoilt, and one day when it refused to get off a chair Gordon throttled it—just like that, apparently without any rage at all.

'He hated civilian life; he couldn't find a niche. He applied for various institutional jobs, he even considered the prison service, but the selectors must have seen he could never work with young civilians, even middle-aged ones, let alone with delinquents.'

Miss Pink said with sympathy, 'The Services are a closed world; it must have been a traumatic experience, for him particularly, to have to come out into—what? A free-for-all?'

'It was shocking: after years, decades, of respect and appreciation, he suddenly found himself being treated like a silly old man by youngsters less than half his age. Climbing was a case in point. Young Army climbers had always deferred to him because of his rank; it was automatic. He was terribly, agonisingly unhappy, like a man who doesn't know what's hit him.

'Suddenly an aunt died and left me quite a bit of money. We bought Glen Shira House. We'd both known Shira before we were married. Things went well for a time—this was in the early sixties, you understand. What he didn't realise was that even Shira was changing, more slowly than the Lake District and Wales, but the climbers were bringing new attitudes, what *he* called decadence. And the crofters changed—or so he maintained. Once, when he was shouting at old MacNeill about tipping in Scarf Geo, MacNeill told him that gentlemen didn't lose their tempers. He was depressed for days. You see, he'd worked hard to get away from what he thought of as a stigma: his birth, the Barnardo's home; being an officer and a gentleman was his peak of achievement, but on the one hand the present youngsters saw no value in what he'd achieved, on the other, an elderly peasant suggested that he was a fraud. That's how he saw it. It was as if his life was crumbling away.'

'You couldn't help,' Miss Pink said. It was a statement, not a question. Obviously Vera had not been able to help.

She said quietly, 'He seemed set on destroying himself. About a year ago he mentioned suicide. He felt persecuted, even by me. He'd confess his fears and all his frustrations and then accuse me of being about to leave him because he was a failure. Success meant so much to him, worldly success, that there were no other values. He saw no point in going on living. Then he'd rage at me, I think mainly because he sensed that I didn't consider success—in his terms—important. I didn't *say* so, but he knew; he isn't thick, you know, not really. I mean, he wasn't.'

There was a disturbance in the water and a seal humped itself out of the sea and settled on a shelf, gleaming like a long wet boulder. The tide was full now, and with the day, the cloud was disintegrating about the peaks of Rum.

'His remorse was worse than his rages,' Vera said coldly, as if she didn't want to get involved again, as if speaking without emotion could keep the thing at a distance. 'It wouldn't have been so bad if he'd had no sense of guilt....' She shook her head helplessly. 'You see why I tried to make Terry go? He was fascinated by her and she was so careless. Gordon had to be handled with kid gloves and—' her voice dropped, '—you had to love him. All Terry saw was what she called—she actually called him!—a dirty old man! And she said he was only pretending to be shocked because she'd been sunbathing. Can you imagine? When she jeered at him that night, she was telling him things about himself that he'd suppressed for all his adult life. She *hurt* him—and she had all the weapons.'

'Except one,' Miss Pink reminded her.

'Yes, except the last. Silly child. It was just Gordon's bad luck that he had to be the one who was goaded too far.'

'No,' Miss Pink said. 'His control was going; it would have happened with another woman, another person, quite soon. He was a victim too.'

'The murder was the end,' Vera told her. 'He was genuinely appalled at what he'd done but that didn't last. Within a couple of days he must have planned how to kill Madge. Planned it, as you said; it wasn't impulsive.' She shook her head in horror. 'And yet there was that crazy reasoning: he'd committed murder but Madge treated it as a minor delinquency, on a par with the nude bathing or poaching, so he killed her as much to punish her as out of self-preservation—because she didn't give the murder its *value*!'

'Did he tell you that?'

'Oh yes; he always tried to explain himself. We talked a long time last evening.... He said she had no moral fibre.'

'You've been in considerable danger yourself.'

'Not until yesterday. While he was comparatively sane, while he cared about appearances, I was safe. He needed me.'

'When did he come to think he didn't need you any more?'

Vera was silent for a moment, considering, then she went on, 'In one way he needed me right to the last. Yesterday morning, after I'd watched him leave for Portree, I was going to go and see Madge as soon as I could get away but Ken came in with the news—and I came to realise how she'd been killed; not the details, of course, but I knew who'd killed her. We talked when he came back from Portree and he threatened to kill himself if I didn't stand by him. I could have given him an alibi for the dinner period on Wednesday, you see: the first time he went to Eas Mor. Ida was in the dining room, Euphemia was turning down beds. I could have said I went in the bar or he came in the kitchen. But I wouldn't do it, not for Madge's murder. Terry's was an accident—' They regarded each other doubtfully and Vera amended that. '*May* have been an accident, but Madge's murder was—' She moved her hand blindly on the turf as if the search for a word was physical. 'Wrong,' she said. 'Monstrous. It was planned.'

From the east, in the direction of the mainland, came a faint and alien sound: a distant engine.

'Something had to be done quickly.' Vera's voice took on a note of urgency. 'There was no time to consider—at that moment. I said I wouldn't give him away.' She shook her head vehemently. 'I would never have given him up to the police, even in these days.'

The drone of the aircraft grew louder and Miss Pink wondered what the searchers were looking for—certainly not two ladies sitting on the shore and contemplating the sea.

'So he asked me to run him out of the glen in the boot of the car or on the floor but I told him I was under suspicion and would be stopped at the ferry if not before. So he said that if I could incriminate myself for long enough to draw their fire just while he managed to get out of the glen, he might be able to get away altogether. He proposed to take the boat and reach some place on the mainland where he'd steal a car. He actually said he'd "steal"—no euphemism. He was out in the open.'

Now they heard the clatter of rotor blades. The helicopter was flying parallel with the coast but some distance out to sea. The seal flopped in the water.

'So you went down and filled the boat.'

'No.'

'No?'

'I brought the can back full.'

'So the boat had no fuel in the tank.'

'It had enough to get here.'

The helicopter, having turned in to Loch Shira, came back and circled the drifting dinghy. Speech was impossible. At length the aircraft dipped away and headed for the glen. Vera stood up and went to the ruin for the rifle.

'I heard two shots,' Miss Pink said.

'Yes?'

'You said you didn't shoot him, and it was dark so unless he was very close to the shore you couldn't have done.' Vera looked politely interested. 'There are no witnesses,' Miss Pink said, for the second time this morning.

'That doesn't matter. He got as far as here, and the fuel ran out. He had no oars and he can't—couldn't swim. I had started along the coast when he left Glen Shira and I had a torch. I heard him calling when I reached the Boat Port.'

'He was calling for help?'

'Yes. He didn't know who the torch belonged to at that point, you see.'

'Go on.'

'He was quite close inshore actually, close enough for communication, but I didn't say anything. I fired the rifle—in the air.'

Miss Pink frowned. 'To let him know who you were?'

She did not answer directly. 'He was quiet for some time and then he started to plead with me. He said that if I didn't get help, or swim out to him, he would drown himself.'

Neither spoke for a while. Oyster catchers were piping, gulls called; out on the water the dinghy rocked unattended, drifting gently shorewards with the current.

'So you fired the second shot—in the air?'

'Then I heard the splash. Of course,' Vera said quietly to the sea, 'it was the only thing he could do in the circumstances. He wanted to die; he just needed a bit of encouragement.'